THE TINY MANSION

Also by Keir Graff

The Matchstick Castle
The Phantom Tower

THE
TINY
MANSION

Keir Graff

G. P. PUTNAM'S SONS

G. P. PUTNAM'S SONS

An imprint of Penguin Random House LLC, New York

First published in the United States of America by G. P. Putnam's Sons,
an imprint of Penguin Random House LLC, 2020
First paperback edition published 2021

Visit us online at penguinrandomhouse.com

THE LIBRARY OF CONGRESS HAS CATALOGED THE HARDCOVER EDITION AS FOLLOWS:
Names: Graff, Keir, 1969– author.
Title: The tiny mansion / Keir Graff.
Description: New York: G. P. Putnam's Sons, [2020] |
Summary: Twelve-year-old Dagmar and her family spend a summer living off-the-grid
in a tiny home parked in the Northern California redwood forest, next door to
an eccentric tech billionaire and his very unusual family.
Identifiers: LCCN 2019050344 | ISBN 9781984813855 (hardcover) | ISBN 9781984813862
Subjects: CYAC: Family life—California—Fiction. | Eccentrics and eccentricities—Fiction. |
Small houses—Fiction. | Wealth—Fiction. | California—Fiction.
Classification: LCC PZ7.G751575 Tin 2020 | DDC [Fic]—dc23
LC record available at https://lccn.loc.gov/2019050344

Printed in the United States of America

ISBN 9781984813879

1 3 5 7 9 10 8 6 4 2

LSC

Design by Suki Boynton
Text set in Arno Pro

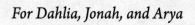

For Dahlia, Jonah, and Arya

CHAPTER ONE
The House in the Forest

The sign on the fence looked like an invitation.

NO TRESPASSING

KEEP OUT

DANGER

THIS MEANS YOU!!!

I know not everyone would see it that way. Some people would see NO TRESPASSING and stop right there. Even people who can ignore KEEP OUT are probably afraid of DANGER. And there are always people who will be fooled by THIS MEANS YOU into thinking someone specifically wrote the sign for them.

But that's not the kind of girl I am.

That's why I had one foot on the tall wire fence, all

ready to find out what was so important that the sign writers didn't want anyone to see it.

The forest of gargantuan redwood trees was dark and wild, and looked like it hadn't been touched in a million years. I almost expected a left-behind dinosaur to come rumbling through, shouldering aside the massive trunks and flattening plants with its giant feet.

I thought of an adjective from my stepmom Leya's word-a-day calendar: *primeval*.

Meaning *of or relating to the earliest ages in the history of the world.*

The calendar's three years out of date. My dad, Trent, snagged it out of a dumpster, but Leya didn't mind. She told him she doesn't really care what day it is, but she does love learning new words.

I hoisted myself up on the fence and started climbing down the other side, just in time to see the gnome trudging through the field I'd just crossed.

"Dagmar!" whined the gnome. "Wait for me!"

I dropped to the ground, hard enough to make my feet hurt, and rubbed the red lines the wires had made on my palms.

Completely oblivious to the crust of snot on his upper lip, the gnome stopped and stared at the sign. "You're not s'posed to go in there," he said, after he finally read it.

The gnome, also known as my five-year-old half brother, Santi, is exactly the kind of person the sign was for.

"Go home, Santi," I told him.

"Okay," he said. "I'll tell them where you are."

"*Don't* tell them where I am. Just tell them you couldn't find me."

"But I did find you," he said, his eyes round as bottle caps.

Welcome to my world.

I turned to go into the trees. "Later, little man."

"WAIT!" he wailed.

I stopped, thinking, *This better be good.*

"I don't know how to get back."

"Are you serious?" I asked.

I don't know why I bothered, because I already knew the answer. Santi's the kind of kid who can't find his way to the bathroom without GPS.

He nodded.

"Wait here, then," I told him.

"I'm afraid."

"Of what?"

He looked around, obviously trying to figure out what to be afraid of.

"Cows?" he said, because the field was fenced and there were a couple of piles of old, dried-up cow poop. At least, I *thought* it was cow poop.

"We haven't seen a single cow since we got here!" I told him.

"They're prob'ly hiding and waiting till I'm alone," he said, starting to sound like he believed it. "They might *stampede*."

I sighed. "If you're so afraid of cows, then come with me."

"I'm afraider of that."

This was getting exasperating. Why didn't Leya ever look after him? But really, he didn't have anything to worry about.

"Then go home, Santi," I said, turning around again, ready to conquer the mysteries of the primeval forest. "You'll be fine."

As I stepped into the waist-high ferns and craned my neck up at the towering redwood trees, I heard whimpering, a digging sound, and then a wail of misery. Putting my hands on my hips, I turned around for the third time and saw Santi stuck under the fence.

Yes, I laughed, but I was also kind of impressed. I didn't think the little guy had it in him.

"Come on," I said, pulling up the bottom of the fence so he could wriggle through. When he stood up, his entire front side was covered in dirt.

"We are gonna get in so much trouble," he said as he followed me into the trees.

. . .

THERE WASN'T A path, so I made sure to take mental pictures of our surroundings as we went along. Exploring is only fun as long as you find your way back. That's something Trent says, whenever we're scouting for unobtanium. *Unobtanium* is what he calls good junk, and sometimes we have to go to strange places to find it: shut-down factories, abandoned industrial sites, and derelict buildings. He calls it recycling, not stealing, because he would never take something someone obviously needed. But a lot of people waste things, so why not put those things to use?

If it's good stuff, like lumber or Sheetrock or wire or nails, he uses it for his handyman service. If it's weird stuff, like old motors or broken electronics or rusty pieces of scrap metal, he gives it to Leya for her sculptures.

I've been all sorts of places with Trent, from water towers to sewer tunnels, but never to a real forest. Sometimes we take little hikes in the hills behind Oakland, where it's kind of woodsy, but I never think I'm going to see dinosaurs there because the old mattresses and beer cans ruin the effect.

"I'm hungry," said Santi, before we'd gone a hundred yards.

"You should have stayed home where there's food," I said.

"I also have to pee," he said.

"There are trees all around us, so take your pick," I said. "I won't watch."

He kept walking, probably trying to think of something else to complain about.

Then we stepped onto a path. It ran left to right, parallel to the fence, so it took me a minute to decide if I wanted to follow it. I was tempted to cross it and go deeper into the forest, but the path seemed more likely to lead us to the reason for NO TRESPASSING.

And maybe there was a good source of unobtanium I could tell Trent about.

We turned left.

We hadn't gone ten yards when two things happened: I felt a little tug on my ankle at the same moment Santi tripped and fell behind me. I turned around to give him a hand up just as a big patch of the forest floor erupted and flew up toward the sky.

If I hadn't turned around, I would have been standing right in the middle of it.

Neither Santi nor I had the words for what happened, but he was the first one to say something.

"Dagmar," he whispered. "This is bad."

My heart was hammering like a paint mixer. High up in the air, a large net was holding a big clump of dirt and leaves and pine needles and pine cones from the place where I had been walking seconds before. The net, made of thick, knotted rope, creaked and turned gently at the end of a long cable that stretched up into the trees above.

It was obviously a trap meant to catch trespassers.

But we had avoided the DANGER.

I pulled Santi to his feet. I could see now that the tug on my ankle had been a piece of twine, a trip wire that triggered the trap. So if I watched my feet, we shouldn't stumble into any more traps.

Unless, of course, there were other kinds we didn't know about.

"Come on," I told him. "Let's keep going."

"I don't wanna!" he said, his eyes leaking all over his face.

"Don't you want to learn how to be brave?" I asked.

He shook his head.

"Then you can go back or wait here."

I kept going down the path, watching carefully for trip wires. I knew he'd start following as soon as I was out of sight. And a little way down the path, I forgot about him completely, because off in the trees, something gleamed like treasure.

I hurried ahead until I could see a huge building made of glass and steel. It looked like a crumpled wad of aluminum foil—no, more like a weird piece of aluminum origami. There wasn't a straight line on it anywhere, and the light green windows reflected the forest around it so I couldn't see inside. I couldn't tell if there even was a front door. Sitting there in the forest, it looked as strange and alien as a spaceship awaiting repairs.

But when some dogs started barking, they didn't sound extraterrestrial at all: they sounded like the mean old mutts Trent and I sometimes found guarding unobtanium.

I saw the dogs a moment after I heard them. As tall as small horses, they streaked out from behind the building and ran to the edge of the clearing, baying and slobbering as they sniffed the air in my direction. Then they took off straight toward me.

"Let's go, Santi!" I yelped as I turned and ran.

But Santi wasn't behind me. Maybe he'd been the smart one, after all.

I raced down the path, wishing I were faster and more graceful. I used to be a great runner, but over the last year I've grown so much that sometimes my bones hurt, and now I run like a giraffe on roller skates. That's what my gym teacher said when she thought I couldn't hear her.

Coming around a bend, I practically steamrollered the gnome, who was sitting cross-legged in the middle of the path like he was meditating. I lost valuable time stopping and yanking him to his feet again.

"*Run*, Santi!" I yelled. "Don't you hear those dogs?"

We plunged off the path toward the fence. Unfortunately, on those short little legs, he was even slower than me.

The dogs were gaining on us, their growls sounding like they came from cavernous, hungry bellies.

Then I heard a noise like a lopsided bowling ball wobbling along an alley. I looked up just in time to see a fat log tumbling down two skids toward us. I had no idea which one of us triggered this trap, but if we didn't get out of the way, it was going to flatten us like bowling pins.

There was no time to think. I leaped, snagged a shoe on the rough bark of the log as it rolled under me, and fell flat on my stomach.

"Jump, Santi!" I yelled, hoping he had enough spring in those stubby legs to get over it, too.

Raising myself on my forearms, I turned and looked: Santi hadn't gotten crushed by the log, but he hadn't exactly cleared it, either. He was running on top of the rolling tree trunk like a lumberjack trying to keep his balance—and if he fell backward, he was going to get pancaked.

"Fall *forward*!" I yelled, and he did, belly flopping on the ground as the log sped toward the dogs, who turned tail and fled.

Scrambling to my feet, I grabbed Santi and pulled

him up. Running was harder on the uneven ground, and we slipped and slid on mossy rocks and rotten wood. Even worse, I think I swallowed a bug.

"This is all your fault!" he panted as we ran. "The sign warned us!"

I didn't waste my breath answering. Instead, I concentrated on putting one foot in front of the other.

Just as the fence came in view, the barking started again.

As it got louder, I heard a human voice: "After them! Don't let them get away!"

Well, we were going to get away or die trying.

This section of the fence was half buried in the ground, so the gnome couldn't go under. Before he could think of a reason to be scared, I grabbed him under the arms and half lifted, half threw him to the top of the fence, where he hung like a big sack of flour. Then I climbed over the top and wedged my feet into the wires so I could help him to the other side.

We dropped to the ground right as the two hounds of heck broke out of the undergrowth, charging straight for us, their teeth snapping like crocodile jaws.

"Come on, Santi!" I pleaded.

We took off in a crouching run and threw ourselves down behind a big bush.

Then we heard the voice again.

"Heel!" it said.

Peeking out, I saw the two dogs trot away and sit next to a boy with dark hair and a scowling face. He was shorter than me but was probably about my age, and he might have been cute if I liked boys, which I don't. My friends at school probably would have said he looked like some movie star I'd never heard of, but all I noticed was his frown and the fact that his hair was perfectly combed.

He walked up to the fence and peered through, looking for us. I ducked down and put my finger to my lips so Santi wouldn't break the silence and give away our location by saying something brilliant like "I peed my pants!"

We crouched behind the bush for a long time, so long that I started to worry the boy had climbed the fence or opened a gate for his monster dogs. We didn't hear them coming, but we didn't hear them leave, either. Finally, I got up my courage and looked.

They were gone.

CHAPTER TWO
The Tiny Mansion

Two weeks earlier, I'd come home to find a tiny red house parked at the curb outside our apartment building in Oakland. It was the second-to-last day of school, and everything was copacetic (*copacetic: in excellent order*)— or at least as normal as things ever got in my mixed-up family. True, we had been eating Crock-Pot beans for a whole week, and Santi's rocket-powered butt was making the bedroom we shared smell so bad my eyes still water just thinking about it. Also true, Leya said if I wanted new summer clothes, I'd have to pick them out at the Salvation Army. And, yes, it was our third apartment in the last eighteen months. But summer was almost here, and I was looking forward to hanging out with my friends when I wasn't hunting unobtanium with Trent.

But there was the house. I recognized it right away, of

course, because Trent had been building it for a while. It wasn't like one of his usual projects, where he would fix somebody's porch or plumbing with unobtanium parts and then get paid in backyard eggs and veggies or some other kind of barter. This one was for two customers who had good jobs and wanted a little weekend house but hadn't decided where to put it yet. They wanted it to be really nice, so Trent built it with fresh lumber and all-new hardware, even windows that came already made in a box. Every now and then I'd go to the warehouse where he kept it and watch him work, sometimes helping if he let me.

I really loved it. Even though the whole thing was smaller than our living room, it was totally adorable, with red-shingled sides, a sloped roof, and even little window boxes for flowers. It was so small inside that it was hard to turn around without bumping into yourself, but everything was perfectly designed, and let's face it: it was much better quality than anyplace I'd ever lived.

A lot of times I wished Trent and I had a place just like that for ourselves, where we could go and hang out without Leya and the gnome. Don't get me wrong, Leya is mostly nice to me, and Santi isn't any dumber than your average five-year-old, but I never asked for a second mom and a new brother after Trent and Kristen (that's my real mom) decided to "consciously uncouple." That's what they called it instead of *divorce*. I think they hoped that, if they didn't use the *d*-word, I wouldn't feel so bad about it.

They were nice to each other while they uncoupled, and nicer than usual to me. But words for things aren't as important as what actually happens, and the end result was that Trent married Leya, they had Santi, and we lived in crummy apartments while Kristen traveled the world wearing suits and using three different cell phones for some reason. She sent us money, but Trent has never been good with money. I'm guessing that's part of the reason they uncoupled.

When I was a little kid, Trent and Kristen told me to call them by their first names because they said *Dad* and *Mom* were "loaded with gender expectations." And I suppose Trent is in some ways a little more like a mom and Kristen is more like a dad, even though none of them—Leya included—act like any of the other parents I know. The good part about living with Trent is that he lets me wear anything I want and eat as much as I like. The bad part is that sometimes it's just plain embarrassing to be so poor and have such weird parents. At Kristen's condo in San Francisco, everything is new, everything works, and we never have to add up how much the meal costs before we order takeout.

Then again, Kristen's condo is empty most of the time. She swears she'll be back from Dubai before

Christmas, but until then, all we can do is text and talk on the phone.

The front door of the tiny red house opened, and Trent's head poked out, beard first, curly hair last.

"Hey, Dagmar," he said. "How was school?"

As a rule, I refuse to answer general questions, so I didn't. Instead, I asked him a very specific one: "What's this doing here?"

He didn't answer right away, which wasn't a good sign.

"Is it done?" I asked.

"It's done all right," he said. "Come in and take a look!"

I hopped up to the tiny porch and went in the narrow door, careful not to bump into him. Trent had to move out of the way so I could squeeze into the living room, which was really about the size of a big closet, and even though he flattened himself against the wall, I still tripped over his feet.

It wasn't his feet's fault—it was mine. I'm not too bad outside, where I have room to move, but inside, I feel like a giraffe in a shop that sells teacups and tripping hazards.

"You okay, Dag?" asked Trent, rubbing my shoulders after he caught me.

I nodded and started looking around. It really was finally done, and it looked great. After the living room came a short hall, off of which were a bathroom, a storage closet, and a ladder leading up to the sleeping loft. Then you came to the kitchen, and that was the end of the house.

If you've never been in a tiny house, all I can say is that they're like 3-D puzzles where everything fits neatly together. And that's great if you're a puzzle kind of person. If you're *not* a puzzle kind of person, all you can think about is the fact that, once you take it all apart, there's only one way to put it back together and you won't be able to remember how to do it.

Suddenly, instead of admiring the way the spice rack folded up under the kitchen cabinet (notice I didn't say *cabinets*) or the way the breakfast bar doubled as an ironing board and a workbench, I felt claustrophobic (*suffering from an extreme or irrational fear of confined places*).

"So, why is this here?" I asked. "Are you delivering it to the clients?"

He rubbed his thumb against the windowsill, and I could picture him working on it, sanding the wood until it was as smooth as a kitten's paw, even if nobody would ever notice how much effort he put into it.

"This house belongs to us now," he said finally.

"That's . . . good?" I asked while I tried to figure out if it actually was.

"I think so," he said, even though he still wasn't looking at me. "I built it using money your mom sent, and the customers were supposed to pay me the full price last month so we'd get all the money back and more. But something happened, and now they say they can't pay."

"Can you sell it to someone else?" I asked.

"I could, but we're a little behind on rent and we need to leave our apartment. So, we're going to live in this for a while."

"All of us?"

Trent laughed. "Of course, all of us. Did you think we'd leave Leya and Santi behind?"

Even though that was a specific question, I decided it was probably better if I didn't answer it.

"It's so . . . small," I said instead.

"Bigger isn't necessarily better," he said. "Think of it as your tiny mansion."

OXYMORON: *a figure of speech containing apparently contradictory terms.*

"Where will we put it? We can't leave it here in the street."

"No, we can't. We'll probably head up north. It'll be like camping—a summer adventure. You and Santi can help decide where."

Now I was starting to panic. Living in a tiny house—excuse me, *mansion*—was one thing. I've lived in some

17

lousy places, and I'm tough enough that I don't complain about square footage. But leaving Oakland and my friends? Imani's birthday party was in seventeen days, and she had asked Olivia and me to help plan it. Never mind all the stuff we were going to do for fun now that we were done with seventh grade.

"You said we would live in this for 'a while,'" I told him. "How long is that?"

Trent shrugged. "I honestly don't know, Dagmar. Maybe a few months . . . or maybe forever if we like it. But probably just until we get back on our feet."

All I meant to do was leave the kitchen so I could go out to the sidewalk and catch my breath before I screamed. But when I turned to go, I crashed into a wall of hanging pans, knocking a bunch of them down, which sounded like gangs of garbagemen having a trash-can fight.

Trent frowned at the hooks I had broken off, then took the multi-tool off his belt and got to work.

"Don't worry, we can fix this," he said.

Unfortunately, some things can't be put back together with a screwdriver.

CHAPTER THREE
A Million Miles from Oakland

Santi, of course, told Trent and Leya about the deadly traps and barking dogs.

Even though I'd told him not to, I'd forgotten to make him promise, and even if he had promised, that's just the way he is: words leave his mouth the moment thoughts are formed in his brain. I think he's afraid that if he keeps the thoughts in, they'll die of loneliness.

"Where did this happen?" demanded Leya. Dropping her gardening tools, she had rushed over to Santi and examined him like she expected to find broken bones or a tree branch sticking out of his head.

Trent put down the rock he was fitting into a wall, wiped his hands on his shorts, and walked toward us.

"On the other side of the fence," said Santi. "The one with the big sign on it."

"We were hunting unobtanium," I said, defending myself.

"You should have asked me to come along," said Trent.

"And you shouldn't have taken Santi with you," said Leya, giving me an accusing look.

"I didn't take him," I told her. "He followed me. If you don't want him following me, you should put him on a leash!"

"Dagmar, that's no way to talk about your brother," Trent scolded me.

"*Half* brother," I corrected him. "Anyway, the point is that there's a primeval forest and a house inside it that looks like a spaceship. You should come check it out!"

Trent loves trespassing to find cool stuff, and he's not particularly worried about danger, so I knew he would be interested. But instead of saying, *Let's go!* he looked at Leya.

She shook her head. "And what if someone discovers us here?"

"What does she mean by that?" I demanded.

"Nothing, Dag," said Trent with a sigh. "But if they're booby-trapping their yard—"

Santi laughed when Trent said *booby*, but we all ignored him.

"—it sounds like they really want their privacy. Besides, if it's an occupied home, we can't look for unobtanium."

"We don't know for sure it's occupied," I said, even though the boy with the dogs probably lived there.

"We're enjoying our privacy, too," he said, "so let's all keep to our own side of the fence for now."

Santi nodded like he was relieved he wouldn't have to go into the woods again, even though nobody made him do it the first time.

"That's for the bestest," he said as Leya led him up to the tiny house for a carrot-carob bar or some other allegedly delicious snack. She seemed to think every problem could be solved by eating healthy food.

ALLEGED: questionably true.

I looked at Trent, the guy who had never seen a fence he didn't want to climb, cut, or crawl under, and wondered what exactly was going on.

"Since you're back, you may as well take care of your chores," he said, smoothing his beard, his eyes revealing nothing about what he was thinking.

"Fine," I said, without giving him any idea what I was thinking, either.

I DIDN'T DO my chores right away. I wanted to avoid Leya and Santi, so I found some shade and waited while she took him inside.

Leya had named the house Helen Wheels. Before we left Oakland, she'd painted the name on a small wooden sign and nailed it next to the front door. But as soon as we arrived here, Trent had jammed rocks on either side of the tires and propped the trailer up on jacks and cinder blocks. Helen wasn't going anywhere on those wheels.

Just below the road and hidden from passing cars, she was slightly uphill from what Trent called our "compound" even though it didn't exactly meet the definition of *a fenced or walled-in area containing a group of buildings*. In front of the house was a dining area shaded by an old tarp, and in front of that, four vintage aluminum-tube-and-nylon-webbing lawn chairs circled a stone fire ring. We'd been there ten days and hadn't had a single marshmallow roast because everything was so hot and dry that Trent and Leya said we might start a forest fire—and anyway, Leya refused to buy marshmallows. I made sure we had plenty of firewood just in case, but it didn't look like it was going to rain anytime soon.

A little way off was Leya's garden, and scattered around

were various other projects she had started, like an art installation made of fabric that was torn and twisted and knotted into a small grove of trees. Sometimes Leya's art was cool, like when she used old record players to make this weird thing that looked like a break-dancing robot, and sometimes I couldn't really understand it, like when she balled up a thousand plastic shopping bags and piled them in the corner of a warehouse. But she was always making stuff and said art belonged in the real world, not museums.

Trent was always making stuff, too, but his stuff was more practical, like bookshelves, cabinets, and tiny houses. He may not have been a good businessman, but he was a hard worker and liked to keep busy, which was probably why he started making a wall out of rocks shortly after we arrived, even if the wall didn't do anything besides look nice.

Finally, Santi came outside with carob smeared all over his eating hole, and when Leya followed, I went inside to start my chores. First, I crawled up the ladder to the sleeping loft, took the sheets off their beds, and threw them downstairs before carrying them outside to the clothesline strung between two trees. Since we didn't have a washing machine, I was supposed to hang the sheets outside every day to keep them fresh.

Then I grabbed the big plastic bucket and the large

watering can and carried them to the pump. The creek down by the pasture barely had enough water in it to make mud, but Trent had discovered an old pump next to a caved-in pioneer house, and the pump, if you worked it hard enough, brought up some water that wasn't half bad.

Even though we'd only been gone a week and a half and were just a few hours away from Oakland, it felt more like a year and a million miles. Trent and Leya had asked Santi and me to help pick our destination, but that didn't work at all. None of Santi's suggestions—Disneyland, Yosemite, Hawaii—were even remotely realistic, and I couldn't help out because I was too busy sending SOS messages.

Run away! texted Imani. **You can live in my closet!**

Which would have been great except for the fact that her closet was about two feet deep and I would have had to sleep standing up.

Make the best of it, texted Kristen. **Don't you want to try camping?**

Apparently, Trent had told her we were going on a long camping trip. Without bothering to add any of the other embarrassing details.

In the end, we just headed north to the redwoods, with me riding shotgun in Trent's old pickup truck while Leya and Santi rode behind in the house, taking one winding road after another until we found a place that Trent said was perfect, even though it obviously wasn't an actual campground.

Maybe it was perfect for them, but I was mad about leaving my friends, mad about having to spend all my time with the gnome, and mad that every time I turned around inside, I knocked something over. On the second day, while I watched Leya hoe the dirt and plant seedlings for a vegetable garden, I realized how to get home. She obviously planned to stay awhile, so I had to make everyone want to go home as much as I did. I had to make everyone as miserable as I was.

I had to sabotage summer.

SABOTAGE: 1) Destruction of an employer's property or disruption of production by discontented workers. 2) Destructive or obstructive action carried out by non-soldiers to hinder a nation's war effort. 3) (a) An action intended to impair or damage. (b) Intentional subversion.

This was definitely a case of 3(b) sabotage, although I guessed there would be a little 3(a) along the way.

I had to look up *subversion* in Leya's paperback dictionary: *an organized effort to overthrow or undermine a government by persons working secretly from within.*

A family was a form of government, right? And when the leaders, Trent and Leya, lacked the consent of the governed, namely me, it was time to change the course of history.

After waving away a couple of wasps that were hanging around the abandoned house, I worked the pump until the water started flowing. Then I put a few inches of water in the bucket and the watering can—much less than I really needed—and carried them back to Leya's garden.

Working my way down the furrowed rows of tomatoes, peas, carrots, and other vegetables she'd planted, I sprinkled just enough water on the leaves to make it look like I had done my chore while the dry gray dirt greedily sucked down any stray drops. The garden wasn't growing well at all. Leya and Trent blamed the wilted, withered plants on the never-ending heat, but I knew the real reason.

She had planted seedlings, but I was growing unhappiness. It was only a matter of time before the two of them decided to give up and go home.

CHAPTER FOUR
Blake Berthold

All day, the compound felt hot as a frying pan and as boring as a black-and-white movie. But finally the sun started to go down, and when it did, the shadows of the trees felt like cool water. I was outside, trying to read a book and wishing my phone got reception, when I heard a snuffling sound.

"Wipe your nose, Santi," I said, without taking my eyes off the page.

But he didn't answer. Then I realized there were two noses making the same sound—snuffling in stereo—and looked up.

The dogs from the forest were padding into our compound with their heads alert and their noses working furiously. They were camel-colored, with black faces and lolling pink tongues. And they were *huge*. Maybe not camel-*sized*, but close.

Behind them strolled their owner, his hair a black slash across his forehead and his eyes and eyebrows making dark lines of their own.

I hated him on sight.

First of all, he walked in like he owned the place, looking everything over like he had all the time in the world. And when Leya poked her head out of her art installation—the thicket where she was tying more fabric to branches—he didn't even answer her friendly hello.

Trent was in the bed of the truck, checking the big plastic tubs that held our dry food supply. He's run into so many guard dogs that it's made him extra careful around canines, which is probably why he hopped down right away and went over to the boy: to make sure we were all safe.

"Nice dogs," he said. "Are those mastiffs?"

The boy nodded and kept moving toward me—then past me—straight to Helen Wheels. He stared at it like an archaeologist discovering a mud hut made by intelligent apes.

ARCHAEOLOGIST: *scientist who studies the material remains of past human life and antiquities.*

ANTIQUITIES: *relics or monuments of ancient times.*

I put my book down, stood up, and joined Trent in walking after him. Santi, who had been digging in the dirt with a stick, ran over to Leya and tried to climb into her lap even though she was standing up.

"I'm Trent," said Trent. "And this is Dagmar," he added, pointing to me.

The boy looked at us blankly and climbed the steps to Helen Wheels. His dogs were between us, so we didn't exactly feel encouraged to follow.

"Make yourself at home," I said sarcastically.

He went inside for a self-guided tour while the dogs roamed around, sniffing everything and lifting their legs to pee on a couple of carefully selected trees.

"I don't like these dogs," said Leya, holding Santi protectively, while Santi held on to his stick like it might do him some good if the dogs decided to attack.

Trent frowned. He obviously wasn't crazy about the dogs or the boy, but unlike me, it's really hard to make him mad. He tends to trust people until it's too late—which probably had something to do with why we were living in Helen Wheels in the boonies instead of an apartment in the city.

Finally, the boy came out of our house. He even said something.

"You guys really live here?"

I wasn't sure if I was more mad than embarrassed,

or more embarrassed than mad. I felt like someone had seen me in my underwear. I wanted to say something smart like, *It speaks!* or *At least I don't live in a giant ball of aluminum foil,* but I couldn't get the words out. And even if he lived in a giant ball of aluminum foil and I lived in a house the size of a walk-in closet, we obviously had one thing in common: neither of us could believe a whole family lived in such a tiny home.

But why would a kid who lived in a real mansion be so interested in a house so small the word *mansion* was a joke?

"We're just stopping by," said Trent, conveniently ignoring the fact that we had planted a garden and started building a stone wall and were now turning the bushes into art. "Is this your land?"

The boy shook his head and came down the steps. I started wondering if words somehow hurt his throat.

Trent moved closer, and I could tell he wasn't going to let the kid go without getting at least a few answers. I moved closer, too, so it would be harder for him to escape.

Then I felt a wet nose on the back of my bare leg and jumped, making an embarrassing *EEEP!* sound.

The dog who nosed me gave me a big lick, I guess trying to see how I tasted, and I squirmed away. The boy whistled, and both dogs heeled.

"What's your name?" asked Trent.

"Blake."

"How old are you?" I added.

"Twelve."

"What are your parents' names?" asked Leya, coming over with Santi hiding behind her legs.

"Reynold and Anjali Berthold," he said with a scowl.

Trent and Leya looked at each other, like they recognized those names, even though they seemed totally random to me. I couldn't understand why they were being so calm about this trespasser! I wished we had our own dogs—bigger, meaner, and more of them—so we could chase him off of our land.

I know it wasn't really our land, but you get the point.

But I didn't have to chase Blake Berthold away, because he left just as suddenly as he arrived. All he had to do was whistle again, and his dogs loped down toward the creek, sniffing and slobbering, while he strolled along behind them without looking back once.

"Did you hear that? *Reynold Berthold*," said Trent, once Blake was out of sight.

He said the name like he'd discovered we were living next door to Bruce Wayne, but it didn't mean anything to me.

"Who's that?" I asked with a shrug.

"He's a huge tech guy, or was," said Leya. "He

invented some really important stuff and made a billion dollars and then just disappeared."

"What did he invent?" asked Santi. It always surprised me when I found out he was listening.

"Something to do with computers, but I never really knew what," said Trent.

"Stuff that's not even real, in a way," added Leya. "Computer codes and processes that connect different devices together, I think mainly for surveillance and so-called 'smart homes' that do everything for you. He changed life for everyone on the planet without making a single thing you can touch."

Everybody was quiet for a minute while we thought about that. It was weird to know our hideaway in the middle of nowhere was right next to someone who had changed the world.

"I'm going to change life for everyone on the planet by inventing burritos that float in the air so you don't have to hold them and get your hands messy," said Santi, who apparently wasn't having deep thoughts like the rest of us.

"I'll make burritos for dinner if you want," said Leya, "but you're going to have to use two hands like everyone else."

I love a good burrito. In fact, burritos are my favorite food. But Leya's burritos—whole wheat tortillas, brown rice, tofu, carrots, and broccoli—barely qualified. Fortunately, we had avocado, but because Helen Wheels wasn't hooked up to electricity, the fridge wasn't working, and we didn't have cheese or sour cream.

So the less said about dinner, the better.

· · ·

THAT NIGHT, WHILE Trent, Leya, and Santi snuggled up in the sleeping loft, I shook out my sleeping bag and got ready to sleep outside again. It was too hot and stuffy inside, and besides, the one night I did sleep there, I woke up with Santi's finger in my mouth. He was asleep, and it was an accident, but still he gagged me and I almost barfed all over him.

Fortunately, he was afraid of sleeping outside.

The only downside, really, was that in the morning my sleeping bag would be covered in thick spiderwebs. I didn't like to think about the size of the spiders who built them, but so far they hadn't bitten me, so maybe we had an understanding.

Unless they were trying to cocoon me.

Shudder.

In the fire ring I had put the battery-powered star lantern from our old bedroom. It was surprisingly bright, even outside, and as the cylinder slowly rotated, it projected a mosaic of stars all over the compound and the surrounding trees. High overhead, real stars glimmered in the clear night sky, moving too slowly for the eye to see. It was beautiful and peaceful, kind of cozy and vast at the same time.

I thought again about what Leya had said, how Blake's dad had changed the whole world for everyone. I guessed there were different ways of doing that. Like, the guys who invented the airplane obviously made it so eventually everyone could fly, and everyone knew their names. Then again, the person who invented the seat-back tray table also changed life for everyone, because people could eat or read books or whatever without doing it on their laps. But nobody knew his or her name, which seemed unfair.

I didn't want to change the world. I would have been happy with changing even one thing for one person: me. All I wanted was to go home and have life back to normal, with my friends, my phone, and cheese and sour cream when I wanted them.

How long would it take for my brilliant idea to work?

CHAPTER FIVE
An Argument in the Forest

I don't know how long it took me to fall asleep that night, because I was mad and I had growing pains. When you've grown three inches in nine months like me, sometimes your bones just hurt, and it's usually worst right when you're trying to fall asleep. When I finally drifted off, I dreamed Imani and Olivia were in Imani's bedroom, dancing around to some song they obviously really loved but that I'd never heard. When I tried to sing along, I thought they'd laugh because I didn't know the words, but they couldn't even hear me. Worse, they couldn't even *see* me. Somehow I was seeing it all, but I wasn't even there.

That's when I realized the sound I was hearing wasn't a snare drum playing a funky beat but Trent's truck tires popping gravel. My eyes popped open. The sun was up, and I was hot and sweaty inside my sleeping bag.

The truck door slammed, and Trent walked down toward the compound, calling, "Breakfast!"

After checking for spiders, I crawled out of my sleeping bag, breaking a couple of sticky spiderwebs as I made my escape, and followed Trent into Helen Wheels.

He was carrying a box of groceries and a bag of ice he'd gotten at the little store twenty minutes down the road. The groceries included milk, cheese, eggs, and . . . sour cream!

Trent winked at me when he pulled the plastic tub out of the bag. It was his idea of a peace offering, because it was pretty obvious how much I'd hated my burrito the night before. Leya doesn't eat dairy, but the rest of us love it.

I should have just accepted the peace offering and gotten on with things, but my dream about my friends was so real it made my stomach ache. So I ignored him, even though I could tell it hurt his feelings. If I was going to win the war through sabotage, I couldn't surrender that easily.

I acted normal while Trent made breakfast. I like his cooking better than Leya's because, even though he doesn't know how to make as many things as she does, he makes them normally. Using the propane stove in

Helen Wheels, he fried some onions and green peppers before scrambling a big bunch of eggs to make breakfast burritos. I topped mine with cheese, salsa, avocado, and a giant glob of sour cream.

Burritos are definitely the biggest brick in our family's food pyramid. But really, anything rolled up in a tortilla can be a burrito, so we still have lots of variety.

After breakfast, everyone else went to take showers, which meant dumping buckets of water over their heads at the pump. Helen Wheels did have the world's tiniest shower stall, but since it wasn't hooked up to a water line, it was useless in our current situation.

While they were gone, I committed another act of sabotage.

I was glad Santi enjoyed a big glass of milk at breakfast, because he sure wasn't going to like the next one. I poured three big glugs of vinegar into the milk jug, screwed the cap on, and gave it a good shake before putting it back in the cooler. Then I went outside and scooped up a handful of the smallest gravel I could find. I mixed that into the granola, because everyone in the family ate that all day long whenever they got hungry.

While I was getting the gravel, I saw a fat slug under a leaf, so I went back and got it and put it in Santi's shoe.

After everyone came back from the pump, their hair dripping, I changed into my swimsuit, took my towel, the bucket, and the watering can, and headed over to take my turn. We had biodegradable soap that also doubled as shampoo, even though it left my hair feeling dry and tangled.

At the pump, I filled the bucket and dumped it over myself. The water was ice-cold, but I liked the shivery feeling while I soaped myself up and the way my long, wet hair felt on the back of my neck. I knew I would be hot and sweating before long because, once again, there wasn't a cloud in the sky. It took two more bucketfuls to rinse myself off. I'm not sure how clean I really got, because I couldn't scrub under my swimsuit and I wasn't about to take it off outside, even if I was alone.

I pumped a little bit of water into the bucket and watering can and carried them back to Leya's garden. Obviously, sour milk and gritty granola alone wouldn't overthrow the government. I needed to keep attacking on multiple fronts.

As I went down the neatly furrowed rows of Leya's vegetable garden, I thought of a reason to be mad each time I sprinkled a tiny amount of water on the leaves.

This is for my friends, I thought.

And this is for making me miss Imani's birthday party.

Finally, I just emptied the bucket and the watering can on the ground. *And this is for everything else!*

I looked down. The dirt caked on my wet feet made it look like I was wearing brown socks.

Just as I headed back to Helen Wheels, I heard a wail of despair.

Santi had found the slug.

■ ■ ■

IT SEEMED LIKE a good time to get lost, so while Trent and Leya explained to Santi that slug goo wasn't flesh-eating poison and promised he could hold a funeral for the shell-less mollusk, I pulled on shorts and a T-shirt over my swimsuit and headed out.

I went down the path to the pasture, keeping my eyes and ears open for any roving bovines, and then went straight for the fence around Blake Berthold's forest.

I wondered how serious Trent was when he said we shouldn't go in. Was he just saying that to make Leya feel better? And did he only mean that I shouldn't go in with Santi? That was reasonable, and I didn't want to take Santi again, anyway. The little man just slowed me down and was likely to set off traps.

I stared at the NO TRESPASSING sign. I paced up and down, eyeballing the trees. I listened for the snuffling of the big dogs.

I made up my mind when I heard Santi coming down the path.

"D-D-Dagmar!" he called, still half crying. "Come help bury the slug!"

That did it.

Before he could reach the pasture and see me, I scrambled up the fence, dropped down on the other side, and hid behind a big redwood.

"Dagmar!" he yelled. "There wasn't very much left, but we wiped it on a leaf, and now we're gonna bury it!"

I didn't answer, obviously. It didn't take long before he went back, probably to tell Trent and Leya I'd run away or something. If I was lucky, he'd get distracted by an interesting rock and forget to mention it.

I moved deeper into the woods. This time, when I reached the path, I turned right, away from Blake's house. I was curious to see it up close, but I wasn't exactly excited to encounter him or his dogs again. And who knew what else I would find?

I walked beside the path, not on it, moving slowly and keeping my eyes peeled for anti-trespassing devices. I saw a new one, too: a big bag of rocks hanging high in a tree that would drop and crush anyone unlucky enough to walk underneath.

Who made all these traps? And why? They didn't fit with the futuristic fortress I'd seen through the trees.

And if Blake's dad really was a tech wizard, it seemed like he would have protected his property with drones, lasers, and robots, not ropes and logs.

The forest got darker as the canopy grew thicker overhead. The path was so overgrown with ferns and things it was hard to follow—making it hard to spot trip wires or other triggers, if there were any.

I stopped, suddenly not sure I wanted to keep going. Honestly, I was afraid of getting lost. A forest isn't like an abandoned factory, where you always know the way out.

And then I heard voices.

"Step back on your side!" shouted a man.

"I am on my side! And stop putting traps on my land!" bellowed another man.

"Don't forget what we came here to talk about!" pleaded a woman. "What's going to happen isn't fair!"

I couldn't understand what they said next, because they quieted down, but I could tell which direction the voices were coming from. Dropping to all fours so they wouldn't see me, I crawled toward the argument. It felt like a whole other world under the ferns that covered the forest floor: I saw spiders and centipedes and a slug I hoped wasn't related to the one I put in Santi's shoe. I also saw a bunch of pine cones, some tiny and some as big as footballs, making me wonder if people who walked through really old forests should wear helmets.

I went up a little hill and hid behind a fallen log, where I was able to see who was talking. There were two men and one woman, and they looked almost as out of place as the spaceship house. One of the men was dressed like he worked in an office, wearing gray slacks and a crisp white shirt. The other man looked like a lumberjack in jeans and a plaid shirt. The woman was wearing huge sunglasses and a scarf around her head, like a movie star who didn't want to be recognized by her adoring public.

Even though they weren't yelling at the moment, they all looked mad enough to start hitting. They kept interrupting each other, rolling their eyes, and throwing up their hands in exasperation. The last time I'd seen behavior like that was when Santi was with a group of his friends and they all started arguing. In other words, these people were acting like five-year-olds.

Concentrating hard, every now and then I caught just a little bit of what they were saying.

". . . act like no one else exists . . ." said the movie star.

". . . want it all for yourself . . ." said the lumberjack.

"It's mine," said the businessman, practically spitting. "All mine!"

I had just decided to go around the log and work my way closer when someone touched my shoulder.

CHAPTER SIX
The Smart House

I almost screamed. And then I nearly decked the person who touched me.

I would have, too, if he hadn't ducked. When someone scares me enough, my initial reaction is to swing first and ask questions later.

Blake gave me a weird look, like he thought it was funny I'd tried to punch him. On either side of him, his dogs watched me, panting, their big tongues hanging out like short pink neckties.

"Trespasser," he said.

"I got lost," I said, keeping my voice down because I didn't want the grown-ups to hear us. It was a dumb thing to say, but I didn't want to admit he was right.

"Liar," he said, like it was no big deal.

"There must be a place where there's no fence, because I didn't even realize I was on your land," I said, doubling down since he'd already called me a liar.

Blake smirked. "I watched you climb the fence. We have cameras in the trees."

I didn't know what to say to that. It gave me a weird feeling to think this beautiful forest had primitive but deadly traps *and* high-tech surveillance equipment. *Was it a real forest, or was it some fake Disney version?*

Before I could decide how to answer, Blake pulled something out of his pants pocket and turned so I couldn't see it. I heard a *snick snick* sound, then a *sizzle*, and then he turned back toward me with a big grin on his face.

He was holding a finger-sized firecracker with a burning fuse.

"What are you—"

Before I could say *doing*, he tossed the firecracker over the log and disappeared into the trees with the dogs on his heels. I froze, feeling caught, and hadn't taken a step when the firecracker exploded with a *POW!*

I peeked over the top of the log. The three grown-ups were looking right at my hiding place.

"Who's there?" called the businessman.

And then they started coming toward me. The lumberjack was in the lead, taking big strides across the forest floor.

I took off running. I probably should have been thinking about how to get out of the forest and back to the compound, but all I wanted to do was find Blake and make up for the punch I'd thrown and missed.

Bushes whipped my legs as I gave chase, zigzagging between tree trunks, some of them wider than Helen Wheels.

Then I saw a dog's tail sticking up over a fallen log like a periscope. I jumped over, arms outstretched, ready to hold Blake down and make him pay.

I did the first part, but before I got to the second part, I heard something that made the hair stand up on the back of my neck: the dogs were growling, low, menacing rumbles that started deep in their bellies.

I froze.

Blake grinned, even though I had his shoulders pinned to the dirt.

"You'd better let me up," he said.

I could hear the grown-ups coming, so I climbed off, and we both wedged ourselves into the opening under the log. The dogs seemed to know what to do and lay down flat, their ears up and alert while Blake patted them soothingly.

Boots crunched nearby. There was a pause and then the wearer of the boots—probably the lumberjack— jumped up on the log, right above our heads.

The dogs looked like they wanted to bolt from their hiding place and start barking, but they were well trained and didn't make a sound.

The lumberjack stomped back and forth on the log, waiting for the others to catch up. Finally, I heard the other man call to him.

"Do you see anyone?"

"No," came the answer.

"I think we all know who it is," said the woman.

In the shadow under the log, I could see Blake grin.

"Let's not jump to conclusions," said the businessman.

Slowly, they moved away. We waited a few more minutes before we crawled out from our hiding place. My breathing still wasn't anywhere close to normal.

"Want to go to my house?" asked Blake.

■ ■ ■

I'M NOT TOTALLY sure why I agreed to go. After all, Blake was rude, arrogant, and unpredictable. His dogs were scary, his forest was dangerous, and the only other people I'd seen on his land acted like they hated each other. And, if the part about the hidden cameras was true, somebody had a bad case of paranoia.

But Blake also seemed to be the only kid in a thirty-mile radius who was my age. And to be honest, spending a boring day at the compound seemed worse than any-thing that could happen with him.

I followed him as he moved confidently through the forest, not using a path, while the dogs roamed around us.

"Who were those people?" I asked.

"My dad, and my aunt and uncle."

"What were they arguing about?"

"They have a business disagreement."

I ducked under a branch and thought about how Kristen once told me her natural habitat was conference centers and hotel rooms. "Why don't they meet in an office or something instead of the middle of a forest?"

"They don't trust each other, so they meet in neu-tral territory. That place where you saw them is the only part of the forest where all their property lines come together."

This was getting weirder and weirder.

"And your dad is Reynold Berthold," I said.

"Yup."

"Who is he, exactly?"

Blake looked at me the way he'd looked at Helen Wheels, like I was a primitive life-form he'd just discov-ered. "You actually don't know? Have you spent your whole life off the grid?"

My face burned, and I could tell I was blushing. Then, to make matters worse, I tripped, and even though

I didn't fall, I had to do this crazy stumble and twirl before I caught my balance.

Blake looked at me and laughed.

"Well, it's not like you know who my dad is, either," I said, steadying myself on a tree trunk.

"But he's not famous, is he?" said Blake.

I thought about turning around right then and there. And maybe I would have, if I'd had any idea how to get back. But the trail was nowhere in sight.

We reached his house just a few minutes later. It was pretty cool, I had to admit.

Then again, *cool* probably is a little weak. According to Leya's word-a-day calendar, the house was prodigious (*causing amazement or wonder*), nonpareil (*having no equal*), and anomalous (*deviating from what is normal, usual, or expected*).

Not that I would have told Blake that.

I really do think the architect's inspiration must have been the crumpled balls of paper containing the unused ideas she threw in the trash—the balls of paper, not the ideas on them. The part of the house I'd seen the day before was the back, and when we went around to the front, there was a garage with a couple futuristic-looking cars inside, and a long driveway that wound off through the trees in the opposite direction of our compound.

Everything in the yard seemed oddly neat and clean, like little robots came out at night to cut the grass and sweep the walks. And when I looked up into the trees, I finally spotted one of the cameras Blake had mentioned. I waved, even though I was tempted to make a much ruder gesture.

"So, what do you think?" asked Blake.

I just shrugged, as if to say, *You've seen one crumpled-aluminum-foil house, you've seen them all.*

He seemed disappointed by my reaction. "All the really cool stuff is inside," he said, opening the front door.

The first thing I noticed was how cold it was. I've never been in a morgue, and I hope to keep it that way, but people are always saying something is *cold as a morgue*, and I guess this is what they mean. My sweat froze, and my arms broke out in goose bumps.

The place was huge, and I'll be honest, the inside reminded me of a spaceship just as much as the outside. Blake gave me a tour of the ground floor, and in every room he demonstrated some futuristic gadget like it made him bored to do it. In the living room, the windows tinted darker or lighter by voice command; in the kitchen, the fridge made its own shopping list and emailed it to the people who delivered the food; and in the family room, screens rose out of nowhere for TV watching, gaming, or computing.

For some reason, all I could think of was Leya's old laptop, covered in stickers, marker, and Santi's gooey fingerprints.

By then I was outright shivering, and I wished I'd brought a sweater—but who wears a sweater in summer?

"We have to keep it cold for all the electronic stuff to work," said Blake when he finally heard my teeth chattering. "This is a smart mansion, and it's all based on technology my dad designed. I haven't even shown you one percent of what it can do. It's run by a computer that could probably launch a spaceship."

"Are you sure this *isn't* a spaceship?" I asked sarcastically.

It seemed like he actually had to think about it.

"Pretty sure," he said.

Then he led me back into what he called the office. It didn't look like a home office; it looked like an office at an actual business. There were half a dozen workstations, each of them with brand-new computers and multiple monitors. In one corner was a glassed-off booth containing a long worktable piled with electronics.

"What is all this for?" I asked.

Blake shrugged. "This is where my dad works on ideas."

Then he sat down at one of the computers and tapped a few buttons. The large computer screen filled with dozens of tiny rectangles. Each rectangle gave a view inside the house, outside the house, or in the forest. One of them, I noticed, showed the whole cow pasture in front of the NO TRESPASSING sign.

Seeing something move, he clicked on one of the rectangles and expanded it to fill the whole screen. In the forest, the businessman was making his way back to the house.

"Time for you to go," Blake told me. "My dad's coming home."

"Wait," I demanded. I still had so many questions. "Why are the woods filled with deadly traps?"

Suddenly, a giant man appeared, almost as tall and wide as the doorway he was standing in. It wasn't Blake's dad. The top of his bald head was polished to a high shine, and he wore a tracksuit so new it was like he'd just taken it out of the shopping bag. His face reminded me of those sculptures on Easter Island: massive, slablike, and hard as rock.

"There are you," he said in a gravelly voice. His accent sounded like he came from Russia or one of the countries around there.

"Busted," groaned Blake.

"I show your friend her home," said the giant.

CHAPTER SEVEN
Setting a Trap

Blake said goodbye, and the large, rectangular man guided me down a stairway and into the garage, where there was a vehicle that didn't look futuristic at all: a large, black SUV with tinted windows. He opened the door to the back seat.

"Get on, please," he said. I guessed he meant *get in*. His English sounded like a work in progress, but he was close enough that I could tell what he meant: he obviously intended to show me *to* my home, not show my home to me.

I didn't budge. "I know how to get home from here," I told him.

"Forest very dangerous," he said, motioning toward the SUV like he was trying to sweep me in. His hands were almost as big as broom heads.

"I can take care of myself," I said, taking a tiny step backward.

He took a big step forward, and it felt like a shadow passing in front of the sun.

"I make sure you get home safe."

Who was I to argue with a bald giant who looked like he was carved out of stone? I climbed in. Like Trent says, sometimes you have to pick your battles.

He got behind the wheel and started the engine. Naturally, the windows stayed up, and the air-conditioning came on full blast. Didn't these people ever get cold?

As we went down the driveway, I leaned forward in my seat.

"So what's your name?" I asked.

"Vladimir," he said.

"And you work for Mr. Berthold?"

"Yes," said Vladimir.

"What do you do, exactly?"

"I am manny," he said with a deep sigh, which was confusing. I guessed he was saying he did *many* things. Like being a bodyguard, for one.

"Do you want to know my name?" I asked.

"Okay," he said, not sounding like he really did.

"It's Dagmar. Do you want to know where I live?"

"I am knowing already."

That was a little creepy, but considering the cameras

in the trees and the computers in their spaceship, the Bertholds could just as easily have had their own satellite, too, that they used to keep an eye on the surrounding landscape. Neither of us said anything else while he drove me back to the compound on winding roads that left the forest and went around it. It was a twenty-minute ride instead of a fifteen-minute walk, which seemed kind of pointless.

When I saw we were almost there, I told Vladimir to pull over and let me out.

"I take you rest of way, is no trouble," he said.

"Thank you, but I'd rather walk."

He looked at me in the rearview mirror and seemed to understand what I really wanted, which was not having to explain to Trent and Leya why I'd arrived home in a big, black SUV with tinted windows.

He pulled over and let me out. I almost said, *Thanks for the ride,* before I remembered I didn't really want it in the first place. So instead I said, "See you later," even though I hoped I wouldn't.

I walked the last few hundred yards up the dirt road while he turned around and drove off. Even though I avoided having Trent and Leya notice *how* I arrived, they still couldn't miss the fact that I'd left going one way and returned from the completely opposite direction. Fortunately, they didn't say anything about it.

The slug funeral was over, and Santi was playing

some made-up game involving rocks, sticks, and pine cones that could talk and fly—I didn't bother asking the rules or the point of the game, because there was a good chance neither existed. Trent was working on his stone wall, which was now about twelve feet long and three feet high and still completely useless. True, it looked nice and the rocks fit together tightly, but the wall still had absolutely no reason to exist.

"You're just in time, Dagmar," said Leya. "Lunch is ready!"

For lunch we were having fresh fruit and granola with milk.

Perfect timing.

I waited until everyone else had been served before taking my bowl and heading off to a lawn chair. I hadn't really thought about the fact that I was sabotaging myself, too.

"I know this is breakfast food," said Leya, pouring herself soy milk instead of real milk, "but the ice in the cooler is melting, so I figured you guys should use up the milk right away."

I lifted my spoon to my mouth, thinking I'd just pretend to take a big bite, but I saw Leya looking at me and smiling, so I had to make it real.

Smiling right back at her, I put the mixture in my mouth and rolled it around.

The sliced peach wasn't bad, but the granola was gritty, and the milk was so vinegary and awful my lips practically puckered back into my head. The moment she turned her head, I spit the whole thing out.

I didn't have to wait long for their reactions.

Trent frowned and looked thoughtful. "Leya, isn't this a little . . . *crunchier* than usual?"

Leya took a small taste. "It's sandy. Somehow we got something in the granola."

Santi, who had taken two big bites before he even started chewing, making his cheeks puff out like a squirrel, went, "BLEAH!!!" and spewed sour, gritty granola all over his lap.

"This is awful tasting and gross!" he wailed.

Trent put his spoon down. "I think he's right. Dagmar, is yours the same?"

I just nodded. I was afraid if I said something, they'd be able to tell from my voice I was lying.

Leya checked our big bin of granola while Trent got the milk out of the cooler and sniffed it. From the look on his face, I could tell he knew the whole jug was ruined.

"Major bummer," said Trent.

He didn't seem all that mad about it, which is one of the things that's frustrating about him: even when he should be mad, you can tell he's thinking, *That's just the way it is.* Honestly, it's like punching a marshmallow.

But if he was Mr. Easygoing, Leya and Santi more than balanced him out. Even though she had no idea how the granola got ruined, Leya was furious and told everyone they could get their own lunch. Santi, still crying over sour milk, told her he needed a carob bar to get the taste out of his mouth, but she wouldn't let him have one, which only made him cry more.

I sliced a peach onto a tortilla smeared with sour cream and rolled it up, making a peach burrito. Honestly, it wasn't half bad.

■ ■ ■

THAT AFTERNOON IT was so hot that even reading a book made me want to fall asleep.

Santi was playing with a stick, as usual. The way he waved it around, you'd think he'd found a lightsaber or a magic sword.

I walked down to the creek and wished it had some water in it so I could go swimming, or wading— unfortunately, the best I could do was get my feet muddy.

Bored, I pulled some thin branches off a willow bush and stripped the leaves. The green twigs were soft and pliable (*bending freely without breaking*), so I wove them into a simple little basket. When a grasshopper landed near me, I sat almost perfectly still, slowly lowering the basket until I could drop it and trap the bug inside. After a frantic effort to get out, it calmed down, and I lifted the basket and cupped the bug in my hands. I got one good look at its alien face before it jumped away and was gone.

Grasshoppers sure are weird-looking.

Then I got another idea.

Without letting anyone see, I borrowed a pocket-knife, pruning shears, and a small handsaw from Trent's toolbox, and an old sheet and some rope from Leya's art supplies. Then I followed a narrow path along the creek until I had the privacy I needed.

First, I cut some branches that were a lot bigger than the twigs I'd played with—these were as thick as Trent's thumb. Once I had a dozen, I leaned them together in a beehive shape and tied them at the top with pieces of torn sheet. Then, using lots of smaller, softer branches, none of them bigger around than my little finger, I weaved in and out around the ribs of my upside-down basket. Here and there, I knotted strips of fabric to strengthen it and hold it together.

When I was done, the whole thing came up to my shoulders, which was perfect.

Next, I tied one end of the rope around the top of the basket and the other end around a small, flat rock, which I threw up and over a horizontal branch. Hauling on the rope, I raised the basket until it was about fifteen feet in the air. If you looked right at it, it would be obvious what it was. But if you walked along with your eyes on the ground, you'd never even notice it because it would blend right into the overgrowth.

Next I tied the rope around a narrow tree trunk while I set my trigger. This was the really hard part. A trip wire would have to be thin so nobody saw it, but it would also have to be strong enough to support the weight of the trap.

Unless . . . the trip wire wasn't a piece of string or rope at all. What if it was actually a stick?

It took a lot of experimenting, but finally I nailed it. I tied the rope to a short, thick stick and wedged it under a tree root that looped out of the ground. When I let go, it held the weight of the basket up in the air. Then I found a long, thin branch and carefully laid it across the trail so one end went between the short stick and the root like a lever. If someone stumbled into the branch, it would knock the short stick out from under the root—and the basket would fall on their head.

And there was only one person I knew who was short enough to fit in it.

CHAPTER EIGHT
Crime and Punishment

The trap worked.

Leading Santi to it was a heck of a lot easier than building it, which was disappointing because I'd hoped for more of a challenge. All I had to do was tell him I'd found a box full of candy in the woods—real candy, made from white sugar, with wrappers and everything. The poor jerk believed me and followed me down the path by the muddy creek. I had to go slowly so he could keep up on those short little legs of his.

When we reached the trap, all I had to do was lift my foot over the trigger stick. He hardly lifts his feet when he walks anyway, so naturally he blundered right into it. I took a mental picture of him looking up, his open mouth forming a perfect O as the big wooden basket plunged down. I wished I'd remembered my phone so I could have had an *actual* picture.

Now he was standing inside, his hands clutching the sticks like a little prisoner, begging me to let him go while I sat on the ground cross-legged and tried to decide what I could make him give me. Unfortunately, he didn't have anything I wanted, and even if he promised to stop being annoying, I didn't think he was capable of keeping that promise.

"Dagmar, let me out!" he begged.

"Not yet," I told him. "I'm thinking."

"What are you thinking 'bout?"

"Leaving you in there until tomorrow."

His eyes bugged out. "No! No! Don't do that! Let me out now! Please, Dagmar!"

The irony was that the basket wasn't really that heavy. I think even Santi was strong enough to lift it if he tried. But he just assumed that, because he was in a trap I'd set for him, I was the only one who could set him free.

IRONY: *something contrary to what was expected and therefore amusing.*

"What will you give me?" I asked.

"You can have . . . my rock collection!" he said desperately.

That was not a tempting offer. His "collection" consisted of ordinary-looking rocks from his favorite places, like Children's Fairyland, the beach, and the yards and alleys behind places we had lived. Honestly, I didn't even know how he remembered which was which.

"Not good enough," I said.

"I'll do your chores," he pleaded.

That would have been a better offer, except for two reasons: one, he wasn't tall or strong enough to do my chores, and two, even if he had been, actually watering the garden would ruin my plan for sabotage.

"It's going to have to be something else," I told him.

Santi's face started shaking like Jell-O, and I knew what was coming next: a full-on geyser. Honestly, that kid cried so much, he must have been constantly dehydrated.

So I wasn't surprised when he started crying. But I was surprised by how loud he was. He tilted his head back like a coyote howling at the moon and let loose a wail that would have drowned out an ambulance.

"Sshh! Sshh!" I tried to shush him, but it was useless.

"LET ME OUT, DAGMAR!" he wailed.

"Fine, I'll let you out," I told him. "Just pipe down!"

But there was no stopping him. If anything, he got louder. I stood up, dusted off the seat of my shorts, and prepared to pull on the rope to lift the trap, disgusted that I wasn't going to get anything good out of him.

And that was how Trent and Leya found us: with me holding the rope and Santi trapped in the basket, crying his eyes out.

If I had any hope that Santi would cover for me, that died in a nanosecond. As they looked from me to the basket and back again, maybe wondering if I was freeing him from some random trap he'd blundered into, Santi stuck his little arm through an opening and pointed an accusing finger straight at me.

"SHE DID THIS," he blubbered, one nostril inflating a snot bubble. "SHE WON'T LET ME OUT!"

...

WHAT FOLLOWED NEXT was surreal (*possessing a dream-like or irrational quality*): the first argument I'd ever seen between Trent and Leya.

It started slowly, because even with Santi flat-out telling them I was guilty, it took a while for Trent to believe it. Leya lifted the basket herself and threw it to one side, smothering Santi in a hug and then checking him over from head to toe to make sure he didn't have a scratch on him. The only thing wrong with him was that his shirt was so wet from tears it needed to be wrung out.

Under the circumstances, it would have been unfair to ask her to compliment my basket-weaving, which in a way reminded me of her art installation.

When she was finally convinced Santi wasn't hurt, she started chewing me out royally.

"What is WRONG with you, Dagmar?" she screeched. "How dare you treat your brother this way?"

"Half brother," I mumbled.

"WHAT?"

"I was only playing," I said.

"Still, probably not very cool, Dag," said Trent.

"Not very COOL?" repeated Leya, turning on him. "Your DAUGHTER trapped our SON like an ANIMAL!"

I was about to point out that five-year-old boys basically were animals, but Trent clearly didn't like what she'd said.

"Whoa, whoa, whoa," he said. "*Our* son but *my* daughter? And you expect them to behave like brother and sister? That's not very cool either, Leya."

"Well, I'm not feeling very cool!" yelled Leya. "I'm upset!"

"All right, I can understand that," said Trent.

Most dads probably would have gotten red in the face and yelled back, but Trent isn't most dads. Like I said: punching a marshmallow.

"You need to punish Dagmar!" demanded Leya.

Trent and I looked at each other. We were both confused. *Punishment* just wasn't really part of our vocabulary, so neither of us knew the definition. He didn't have a lot of rules, so I'd never really broken any. If I made a bad decision, he told me he was disappointed, which made me think about making a different decision the next time. Sometimes I actually did.

"Now!" added Leya.

I could see Trent basically agreed with her that I'd done something wrong. But I could also tell he had no idea how to punish me. He couldn't take away my phone, because my phone didn't work out here. He couldn't take away my allowance, because there was nowhere for me to spend money even if I did get a regular allowance.

But then finally he figured out the one thing guaranteed to drive me crazy.

"Dagmar," he said, after drawing a deep breath, "I want you to go inside and stay there until we tell you to come out."

• • •

THE TINY HOUSE was hot and stuffy. I could walk from one end to the other in about twelve steps, and that was if I kept my steps short. I poked my head up into the sleeping loft, but that was the hottest part of all, so I flopped down in the living room, which had a little bookcase, a fold-down coffee table, and just enough seating for four skinny people who didn't mind being joined at the hip.

Everyone else was still outside, so at least I had the place to myself. I could hear Trent and Leya continuing their argument outside—she was doing most of the talking, but the quieter he got, the more I knew he was arguing back in his own way—until Trent got in his truck and drove away. I guessed he was going for more milk and ice and granola, but I didn't really know.

Each of us had been allowed two shelves on the skinny bookcase. Leya's books were a mix of novels and biographies of artists I'd never heard of. Trent's were mostly reference books about carpentry and plumbing, although he did have a few political books and even some poetry. Santi had picture books and chapter books, nearly all of them featuring dragons. And my books—well, I don't like to brag, but I have excellent taste in reading, and I had an awesome collection of adventure books and weird novels I'd found at library sales, the Salvation Army, and Little Free Libraries. My favorite one was called *Isolate Islands and Atmospheric Archipelagoes*, by someone named Kingsley van Dash.

Unfortunately, I'd already read all of my books, most of them more than once. I picked up *Isolate Islands* and opened it to chapter one, but I just couldn't get into it. I looked over Trent's and Leya's again, but none of them seemed that interesting.

Just for something to do, I started opening drawers. Mostly they contained normal household stuff like tape and string and spare light bulbs, but one of them was labeled PAPERWORK. Inside I found folders marked BILLS and TAXES and TRENT'S BUSINESS. The first one was full of bills for everything from electricity to doctor's visits to rent, all of them marked at the top with things like PAST DUE and FINAL NOTICE. A couple even had headings like NOTICE OF COLLECTION. I didn't look at all the details, but it seemed like a lot of places charged us extra money just for being late. And an EVICTION NOTICE from our landlord made me realize we hadn't really had a choice about leaving our apartment.

The last folder was full of invoices and receipts and project descriptions, most of them printed in Trent's blocky handwriting on wrinkled notebook paper. But the architectural plans for Helen Wheels had been drawn professionally and printed out on large sheets, which were now folded up and paper-clipped to a contract and an invoice for forty thousand dollars.

I coughed when I saw the number. That was a lot of money! If Trent had been counting on getting that much to pay all the bills, we were in trouble. It made me start to wonder if I was only making things worse by committing sabotage.

But how would things get better if we stayed out here?

Leya was pretty good at arguing, but Kristen was even better. She used to accuse Trent of never dealing with anything, which was both fair and not fair. On the one hand, he worked hard and dealt with people and problems all day long. But he didn't like dealing with boring stuff like money and bills—which I could relate to—so sometimes he let that stuff slide.

And maybe she was a hypocrite, because she got tired of dealing with *him*. After she finished her law degree and business school, she moved across the bay, and ever since then, she'd been traveling all over the world.

HYPOCRITE: *a person who acts in contradiction to her stated beliefs.*

Technically, they had joint custody of me, but Kristen couldn't exactly take me to Dubai for months at a time while I was in school—at least, that's what she said—so I stayed with Trent, who seemed more than happy to deal with me.

I replaced all the bills and papers and put the folders away. If I quit doing the sabotage, then we'd just stay out here and nothing would change. If I kept doing it, and it worked, and Trent and Leya took us back to Oakland, we wouldn't have a place to live. But at least we wouldn't be running away, and we'd have a chance to get back on our feet.

Eventually, Trent returned. I watched through the window as he unloaded something heavy from the back of the truck and carried it behind the house. It looked like a small engine. When he ran an electrical cord from Helen Wheels to it and plugged it in, I realized what it was: a generator.

He saw me looking out the window.

"I figured ice in a cooler isn't enough refrigeration, so this will let us use the fridge. The lights, too."

"Did you buy a cell-phone tower, too?" I asked.

"Sorry, those were out of stock," he said, playing along. "But our cell service is probably going to be cut off soon, anyway."

"Since we don't get reception, how will we know the difference?" I said.

"That's a good point: we won't even notice," he said cheerfully.

I sat down away from the window. He had never liked technology much to begin with, so he was probably happy to be off the grid. And he was obviously settling in for the long haul. So by the time Leya came in a little while later and told me I could go outside to do my chores, I had already decided I was going to do a terrible job again.

CHAPTER NINE
Around the World in Eighty Foods

The next morning, tires sprayed gravel on the road above the compound. That was unusual in itself, because cars only passed a few times a day. What was even more unusual was when the car slid to a stop. Since the compound wasn't visible from the road, no one had ever stopped before. One car door slammed, and then another.

Trent put down the rock he was carrying. After giving Leya a worried look, he started up the hill. I followed him.

Blake stood at the edge of the road, looking down. A moment later he was joined by Vladimir.

"Hello, Blake!" Trent called, as if they were old friends and Blake wasn't the one who'd invaded our privacy and let his dogs pee all over our trees. "Who's your friend?"

They started coming down, but Blake, Mr. No Social Skills, didn't answer, so Vladimir said, "I am Vladimir."

Trent introduced himself and the rest of us, and a moment later, Blake and Vladimir were standing in the middle of the compound while we all stared at them, wondering what to do next.

"Where are your dogs?" I asked.

"At home," Blake said.

"Would either of you like a glass of water?" offered Trent.

Both of them shook their heads. They were such amazing conversationalists, they should have had their own talk show. Leya and Santi stood back suspiciously, as if they didn't quite believe it about the dogs.

"Um . . . why are you here?" I asked.

Blake looked like he had a mouthful of bad food and nowhere to spit it out. Finally he said, "I was wondering . . . if you wanted . . . to go to the mall."

To the mall?

I am not the kind of girl who likes shopping. I think that would be true even if I did have money to spend. Also, I wasn't sure if I believed there *was* a mall, because as far as I could tell, we were surrounded by trees and dead grass and blue sky and suffocating heat. And I definitely didn't like Blake at all.

But going anywhere felt like an adventure, so I

nodded yes. If he wasn't going to use an expressive vocabulary, I didn't have to either.

"Whoa, whoa, whoa," said Trent. "We don't really know the first thing about you, Blake."

"You know who my dad is," said Blake defensively.

"But this isn't your dad."

"Vladimir is my manny," said Blake, using the same word Vladimir had the day before.

"Your *what*?" asked Leya.

"He's like my nanny, but he's a man, so he's a manny," said Blake. "Get it?"

I got it—finally—but I wondered if Vladimir liked it.

"Whenever my parents go out of town, he's not supposed to let me out of his sight," continued Blake.

"Where are your parents now?" I asked.

He shrugged. "Dubai, I think? They'll be home soon."

Maybe they'd run into Kristen, all of them doing whatever it was people did there.

"And why should we trust Dagmar with you, Vladimir?" asked Trent. It surprised me that he was so straightforward about it, but I guessed he wanted to make sure I'd be okay.

Vladimir stood up straight and squared his shoulders, making himself even more rectangular than he already was. "I am highly trained bodyguard. I am black belt in tae kwon do and two-time mixed martial arts champion. In army I was medic. I graduate school for evasive driving and close protection. I am swearing to protect client from all harm using body as shield."

Trent whistled. "Well, that's quite the résumé."

"Do you carry a gun?" asked Leya. "She's not getting in that car if you carry a gun."

Vladimir shook his head. "No. Whole body is weapon."

Trent and Leya looked at each other and then shrugged in unison.

"Well, I don't see why not," said Trent.

"And you can take Santi with you, too," added Leya.

"WHAT?" I said.

"That's a good idea," agreed Trent. "He'll enjoy having a field trip, and he's probably safer with Vladimir than he is with us!"

Blake frowned, but Vladimir nodded sharply. "I protect him also," he said.

"I'm going to the mall! I'm going to the mall!" sang Santi, rubbing his dirty little hands together.

I begged Trent with my eyes. If Santi was going, I wanted to back out.

But the look he gave me in return told me there was no chance of that.

"Have fun!" he said.

THE RIDE TOOK forever. First, we wound along narrow gravel roads. Then we intersected a paved, two-lane road. That took us to a highway. And eventually that took us to a town. Nobody said a word the whole way. Vladimir drove in silence while I looked out the window and Blake and Santi played a game on a screen that came down from the roof of the SUV. Santi had no idea what he was doing, but he loved pushing buttons, so he was happy. It was some kind of cartoony shooting game, and honestly, I think Blake was the one who kept shooting Santi.

I was wearing my cleanest shorts and shirt, and in my pocket I had ten dollars Trent had given me, probably not even enough to buy lunch. I also had my phone, which was dead, and my charger, just in case I had a chance to use an outlet.

Finally, we pulled up to the mall. Vladimir parked away from the rest of the cars, and as we headed for the sprawling building, I could see that he really was a bodyguard. He made sure we stayed close together, and his head rotated constantly so he could watch for danger from all sides.

"Do you really need a bodyguard?" I asked Blake.

"It makes my dad feel better," he said with a shrug. "I think he's really trying to protect me from myself."

Before I could ask what he meant by *that* odd statement, we pushed through the revolving doors and entered the mall. It was an old-fashioned mall, meaning it was all indoors, and after spending more than a week almost entirely outside, it was a shock. First of all, it was as cold as the Bertholds' house. But there was also a creek that smelled like chlorine winding its way down the center of the concourse, and small trees looking sadly up at the skylights, and music coming from hidden speakers. Everybody I saw looked so nicely dressed and put-together that I felt ratty and gross.

Blake held out his hand and said, "Money!"

Vladimir unzipped one of his tracksuit pockets, removed a fat wallet, and counted out ten twenty-dollar bills.

Blake left his palm open. Looking at me and Santi, he said, "What are *they* supposed to spend?"

Vladimir didn't sigh or scold him or close the wallet. He just counted out a lot more money and gave it to Blake, who gave Santi and me little stacks of our own.

While Santi tried to fit all of his in one pocket, I tried to hand mine back to Blake.

"Blake, I can't take this," I said. "I'd never be able to pay you back."

He just started walking into the mall. "You don't have to. There's plenty more where that came from."

When it was truly obvious he wasn't going to accept it, I put the wad of money in my pocket and hurried after him, feeling a weird mix of things. It was nice of him to give us so much cash, but it also made me jealous, or maybe even mad, that he had so much to throw around. It might not mean anything to him, but what he'd just handed me could feed my family for more than a week.

Shopping was weird. Santi wanted to buy everything he saw, and for a while he did, with Blake helping him figure out the amounts and cracking up at all the crap he was getting: a Hello Kitty key chain, a stuffed snail, a plastic grabber with jaws in the shape of a dinosaur head, candy jewelry, a Space Force T-shirt, and other junk. We went in and out of stores for clothes and electronics and knickknacks, and I felt dizzy just looking at it all. Every now and then, Blake would hand Vladimir a shirt or something, and Vladimir would pay for it with a credit card, so Blake didn't even have to dip into the cash in his pocket. And, naturally, Vladimir carried the bags.

"Come on, buy something," said Blake to me.

To make him happy, I bought a couple of paperbacks, even though they didn't seem like books I really wanted to read. He just looked at them and shrugged.

Then we arrived at the food court. The smells were mouthwatering because Trent and Leya never let us have junk food. At all. If you haven't guessed already,

Leya is whole-grain, organic, non-GMO, vegetarian, and no-added-sugar, and tries to make us eat the same way.

Santi turned circles in the middle, like the choices were breaking his brain: burgers, pizza, hot dogs, noodles, sushi, ice cream, and more.

"Are you guys hungry?" asked Blake.

Were we hungry? We were always hungry—and now we had the opportunity to eat food loaded with salt, sugar, grease, fat, and other important food groups Leya didn't allow.

At first, I was just going to get a slice of pizza with sausage and pepperoni, but I was still hungry after eating that, so then I got an order of General Tso's chicken and a Coke. I still had a little room in my stomach, so I topped it off with an Oreo milkshake.

Santi, meanwhile, had accepted Blake's challenge to go "around the world" and get something from every restaurant at the food court. With Blake and Vladimir helping, he covered two trays with cheeseburgers, pizza, noodles, sushi, tacos, gyros—and of course orange soda, donuts, churros, and baklava. Even though he's a stocky little guy, he's only five, so obviously he couldn't come close to eating it all. By the time he took a couple bites of everything he'd ordered, he was completely stuffed.

It made me sad to see all that food go to waste, but Blake thought it was hilarious.

"Are you sure you don't want something else, Santi?" he asked, even though the gnome was leaning back in his chair and trying not to move, like he was afraid his belly was about to pop like an overinflated balloon. "You didn't get any ice cream."

Santi's face was pale, and the words *ice cream* made him tremble, but still, he turned his head toward the ice cream place like a soldier accepting his mission.

"You are *not* getting ice cream," I told him. "Blake, he's had enough."

Blake shrugged, his go-to gesture. I hadn't known him long, but if I'd had to describe him to someone else, I probably would have given them a visual glossary of his nonverbal vocabulary—shrugs, squints, raised eyebrows, blank looks—plus a list of a few one- and two-syllable words. If any of the mall shops sold word-a-day calendars, I was definitely going to buy him the latest one so he could learn to express himself better.

After clearing our table—that is, after Vladimir and I cleared our table while Blake walked away and Santi followed him—we wandered around some more. Santi walked like he'd swallowed a watermelon and was afraid it was going to fall out at any moment. I couldn't find the word-a-day calendar, or anything else I really had to have, and I was starting to feel cold.

"Blake, are we going back soon?" I asked.

He looked over his shoulder at Vladimir, who had fallen behind and was checking out a tracksuit on a mannequin in a store window.

A grin spread slowly across Blake's face—I couldn't decide if it made him look mischievous or evil.

"Nope," he said, pushing me and Santi into the nearest store.

CHAPTER TEN
Mall Runners

"Follow me," said Blake, not giving us much choice because he was pulling our arms. We were in a store selling nutritional supplements, with plastic tubs and jars and pouches of powders and pills and other astronaut food piled everywhere.

I shook him off. "Blake, what are you doing?"

"Just trust me—and hurry."

Even though I had absolutely zero reasons to trust Blake, something about the weirdness of the day—and the fact that we had a bodyguard, and had been spending cash like it was Monopoly money—made my brain go blank. I followed him and Santi did, too.

We ran to the back of the store, past the counter, and into an area that was obviously for employees only. A guy who was as big as Vladimir and wore a muscle shirt so you could see his bulging, veiny arms looked up from his phone and said, "Excuse me, little dudes, but what—"

"We're leaving," said Blake without slowing down.

We went into a stockroom and then pushed through a door I thought might lead outside but instead opened onto a long gray hallway. We piled into the hall, and the door slammed shut behind us.

"Um, Blake, what is going on?" I asked.

His eyes were sparkling. It was the first time I'd seen him look happy or excited.

"We're playing a game," he said. "It's a way to test Vladimir and keep his skills sharp."

"And he knows we're doing this?" I asked.

Blake nodded. "Totally."

Before I could ask any more questions, he started running.

I went after him, but right away had to slow down so Santi could keep up. He had never been fast, and his trip around the world in the food court hadn't added any miles per hour, so he waddled along as best he could, holding his belly like a bowl of soup he was trying not to spill.

We were obviously in a service hallway. Each door we passed was labeled with the name of a different store, and signs and arrows showed the way to garbage dumpsters, loading docks, and the mall security office. I was tempted to run off to security and report my crazy friend.

Wait—*was* he a friend? There was no point jumping to conclusions.

After we passed a half dozen doors, Blake stopped in front of one labeled SALLY SWEET'S SUGAR CELLAR and pulled the door handle. It was locked, and there was a keypad next to it.

While a wheezing Santi started pushing buttons as though he could guess the right combination, Blake pounded on the door and yelled, "I forgot the code!"

"What are you doing?" I asked.

"Vladimir will be right behind us," he said. "We can't stay here."

The door cracked open, and a surprised-looking teenage girl peeked out. "Who are you guys?" she asked, tucking her blond hair into her pink visor.

"We got stuck out here by accident," lied Blake. "We just need to get back into the mall."

"Okay, I guess," said the girl, opening the door wide and letting us in.

We walked through the store, with the girl trailing behind us to make sure we didn't cause any trouble. Normally, the sight of wall-to-wall rainbow-colored candy assortments would have made Santi freak out with excitement, but this time he kept his eyes straight ahead like he was trying to walk through a forest without getting eaten by wolves.

When we got to the front, Blake looked left and right before starting across the concourse. "Vladimir's back in that hallway, with no idea where we—"

And then he froze. Because Vladimir was *not* back in the service hallway. He was stepping out from behind an artificial waterfall and heading toward us. His expression was a mix of smug satisfaction and weary resignation.

"Run!" yelled Blake.

"But he caught us," I said.

"Not yet, he hasn't!" said Blake, taking off. When we didn't follow right away, he turned back and said, "*Come on*, he wants us to make it hard for him."

Santi trotted after Blake. Either he was getting over his stomach bloat or Vladimir was big and scary enough to make him buy into the game.

Was it a game? All I knew was that there was no way I was going to stand there and let Vladimir catch me if Blake and Santi were getting away.

Shoppers stood and stared as we weaved through the crowd, crossed the concourse, and went into a store selling picture frames. Once again, we ran into the back—ignoring the salesperson shouting, "Hey, you can't go in there!"—and went out into a service hallway. Staring at the long row of electronically locked doors, I wondered if Blake's trick would work again.

But this time, he didn't knock on a door.

Because a small electric cart was sitting right in front of us. It had two seats up front and cleaning supplies in the back; mall staff must have used it to get around.

"Get in!" yelled Blake as he climbed behind the wheel.

Santi pulled himself into the passenger seat while I jumped in back with the mops, rags, and bottles of cleaning fluid.

Vladimir threw open the back door of the picture-frame shop just as Blake stepped on the accelerator and we shot forward. The manny was faster than he looked—he may have been a man-mountain, but he had long legs—and he pounded after us, his outstretched hands inches away from the back of the cart. If he grabbed on, I was sure he would dig in his heels and drag us to a halt.

But gradually, we pulled away. Just before we turned a corner, I saw him stop with his hands on his hips and a thoughtful look on his face. I guessed he was already trying to predict our next move.

I wished him luck, because I certainly had no idea what we were doing.

"Whee!" said Santi as Blake wrenched the wheel to

take us around the corner, making the cart go up on two wheels and almost throwing me out of the back.

Then, as Blake slammed the brakes to avoid a head-on collision with a parked, tank-like floor polisher, Santi changed his mind and said, "I'm scared."

A man wearing a uniform and a name badge did a double take as we pulled out to pass the floor polisher. "Hey! Stop!"

But Blake accelerated again, racing the next hundred yards to a large elevator. He drove inside, then leaned out of the cart and pushed the button for the second floor. As the doors closed, I saw the mall worker take a radio off his belt and talk into it, staring at us the whole time.

"He's prob'ly calling the police," said Santi.

"We should let Vladimir catch us and get out of here," I told Blake, thinking this whole thing had gone too far.

"The more complications, the better," said Blake. "We can't make this too easy. He *wants* us to try to escape. Otherwise his job would be boring. Remember, he's trained as a bodyguard, not a babysitter."

"I thought you said your parents hired him to protect you from yourself," I said, remembering what he'd told me earlier.

"But how can he do that, if he doesn't know what I'm capable of?" asked Blake.

Now I was really confused.

The doors opened on a second-floor hallway that looked almost identical to the first-floor hallway. Blake drove out and parked the cart.

"We'd better ditch this, because they'll be looking for it," he said.

The door nearest us was unlabeled and didn't have a keypad. Blake was ready to push through, but when he saw we weren't following him, he stopped and turned around.

"You're not quitting, are you?" he asked accusingly.

"I'm just not totally clear on what we're doing, Blake," I said. "It doesn't feel like you're helping Vladimir protect you—it feels like you're messing with him."

"How could I mess with him? He's a mixed martial arts champion and a war hero in his native Exurbistan. He appreciates a challenge."

"I think he's probably just annoyed."

While Blake and I were arguing, Santi was looking around like he expected Vladimir to smash through the wall and tackle all three of us.

"Come on, Dagmar," he whined. "Let's go before Vladimir gets here."

"Maybe you're just not very good at this," said Blake with a sigh.

Suddenly, my blood felt like lava, and my head felt like it was going to pop off and explode.

Not very good? Not very GOOD?!? How dare this rich kid tell me I wasn't good at running away and hiding—me, Dagmar, who'd sneaked away from dozens of watchmen and guard dogs with Trent.

Fortunately, my head didn't pop off.

"Fine," I said through gritted teeth. "We'll just see who he catches first."

And then I pushed through the door and started sprinting, leaving both of them behind.

CHAPTER ELEVEN
Mall Rollers

I didn't get off to the best start: as soon as the door closed behind me, my feet got tangled and I fell, sliding a good two yards along the highly polished floor. Discombobulated (*upset or confused*) but still aggravated (*angry or displeased*), I scrambled to my feet and kept going.

I was in a hallway that led past the restrooms and a drinking fountain to the upper level of the mall. On this floor, stores lined a balcony that looked down on the shoppers below, and in the distance I could see escalators in a large central atrium. I turned right, mainly because there were fewer shoppers and stores that way. Up here, not all the storefronts had stores inside. Some of them were covered by big wrappers with messages like DREAM RETAIL LOCATION—1,800 SF and FUTURE BUSINESS OPPORTUNITY!

Which gave me an idea: Instead of running around the crowded parts of the mall, why not just hole up somewhere no one ever went? It would be like the time I won a game of hide-and-seek by wedging myself inside the cabinet under the sink until all my friends went home. Although that was kind of a Pyrrhic victory.

PYRRHIC VICTORY: *a battle won at too great a cost to the victor.*

While I considered my options, Blake and Santi came out of the hallway. I pressed myself against the wall until they headed off in the opposite direction. Once they were out of sight, I started checking the empty stores.

The first one was closed off by plate-glass windows and a locked glass door, so it was out of the question. The second had a steel mesh gate going from ceiling to floor—it was locked, too.

But the third one, for some reason, was just closed off by the vinyl banners themselves. Slipping behind them, I found myself in a completely empty store. The counters, cash registers, and shelving had all been removed. I would have thought an abandoned shop would be a great source of unobtanium, but there wasn't even a chair to sit on.

I looked it over in the dim light filtering in from the mall, wondering if I really wanted to hide out until Blake and Santi got caught—it would have been a lot more fun to run around outside. Then I saw an electrical outlet.

I sat down on the floor, took my phone and charger out of my pocket, and plugged in. I didn't even know if the electricity would be turned on, because in most abandoned places the power gets turned off when the bills stop getting paid.

My phone battery was completely drained, so it took a couple minutes, but eventually it started to charge. A few minutes later, I turned it on, and the phone started working.

It completely blew up with notifications. For the first few days after we'd left, Imani, Olivia, and our friends Hailey and Nevaeh had spammed me with a zillion questions: **Are you there yet? Are you there yet?**

And, **What's going on? How's summer?**

And, **Where ARE you, Dagmar?**

You get the idea. Between the four of them, they'd texted me 178 times. That made me feel pretty good. But after a while, because I wasn't answering, they stopped asking. They kept me on the thread as they started messaging about the plans for Imani's birthday party. Imani and I had been friends the longest, and I really liked Olivia, but sometimes I felt like she wanted me to think she was really Imani's best friend, not me. With me gone, Olivia was acting like she was in charge of Imani's birthday party and had even gotten permission to have it at her grandpa's house, where there was a swimming pool and a barbecue grill. The whole thing was going to happen tomorrow, and there was no way I could be there.

It was just like my dream. They were having fun together, but they couldn't see or hear me.

I needed to tell them I was still alive, but before I did, I had to answer Kristen, who had been texting every day asking me to **Please check in**.

She answered after four rings, sounding sleepy. Dubai is twelve hours ahead of California.

"Hi, honey," she croaked.

"Hi, Kristen," I said.

"Hi, *Mom*," she corrected me. After she and Trent uncoupled, she'd changed her mind about the whole first-name thing, but calling her Mom felt weird after so many years.

"I met a guy whose parents are in Dubai, too," I told her.

"Oh, who's that?"

I almost said *Blake Berthold, his dad is Reynold Berthold*, but for some reason I didn't. Well, I know why: because Kristen would have been super excited about the famous connection, and that's what she'd have wanted to talk about. And that's not what I wanted to talk about.

So I said, "Just a kid."

"Oh," she said. "How was camping?"

That was what I wanted to talk about.

"You should ask me, 'How *is* camping,'" I said.

"What do you mean?" she asked, sounding a lot more awake now.

"Things aren't exactly like Trent told you. We got evicted, so now we're living in a forest."

"You're living in a *forest*?" She sounded shocked, which was good. I needed her to be mad at Trent.

"Well, next to a forest," I admitted.

"I don't understand how Trent and Leya could have been evicted. I've been sending money. Are you telling me you're homeless?"

"Trent invested all the money into building a tiny house, but then the people he was building it for didn't pay, and then Trent didn't have enough money to pay all the bills he's behind on, so we're living in the tiny house. Well, they are. I'm camping outside because I can't stand sleeping in the loft with Santi."

She was quiet for a moment, and I wondered what she'd say next. I hoped she was going to come up with a solution to rescue me and save the summer. Like, *I'll be on the next plane home, and we'll fix this.* Or *I'll send him a year's rent right now because I want you moving back to Oakland.*

Instead, she said, "I'll talk to him."

"Well, good luck, because we don't have cell service out there. I'm calling you from a mall right now."

"Then I'll send him a letter."

"We don't exactly have an address, Kristen. We don't even have a mailbox."

"Then tell him to get in touch with me," she said.

If I did *that*, then he'd know I was ratting him out to her, so that would be an absolute last resort. I didn't say anything.

"Is everything okay otherwise?" she asked.

Otherwise? How could she possibly be concerned about *otherwise*? That's when I really knew she wasn't going to rescue me.

"I really want to go back to Oakland, Mom," I said, accidentally forgetting to call her Kristen and getting a little bit mad at myself about it. "Imani and Olivia are going to have a whole summer without me, and I don't even know if we'll still be friends when I get back."

"I'm sorry, Dagmar, but I can't just jump on a plane right now. I promise I'll find a way to get in touch with your dad, and when I do, we'll get things sorted out."

"Can't you just give him more money?"

"It's not that simple, honey."

I held my breath, hoping she wouldn't try to explain why, because I didn't want to hear it.

"Dagmar, are you still there?"

"Sort of," I mumbled.

"Just give me a little time. I'm sorry summer isn't going the way you wanted. Life is complicated right now, isn't it?"

My thumb hovered over the disconnect button.

"Call me anytime," she said. "I'm always here to talk."

"Bye, Kristen," I said, and hung up.

• • •

I HID OUT for another five minutes, texting my friends that I was all right even if I was being held hostage against my will in the boonies. I didn't give them many details because it was too depressing. They had sent pictures of themselves, nothing special, just a bunch of selfies, but seeing them together and happy made me so sad that I deleted them all.

Happy early birthday, Imani! I wrote, adding every party emoji I could think of. **Wish I was there.**

Nobody answered. Maybe they were all at a movie together or something.

Then I heard Santi's voice.

Not speaking words. He was making more of a *wheeeeeeeeee* sound.

I heard the whir of rolling wheels, and his voice got louder and louder and closer and closer—and then started getting quieter again.

Unplugging my phone, which was now at 17 percent, I stuffed it and the charger into my pocket.

Santi's voice was getting closer and louder again: *wheeeeeEEEEEEEEEEE!*

I went to the front of the store and peeked out. Blake was zooming past on one of those long, electric-powered skateboards, and Santi was clinging to his back like a baby monkey—a very big baby monkey.

Vladimir was about thirty yards behind them on a hoverboard. I couldn't see his feet, but that had to be what he was riding, because if it wasn't, he was levitating like an avenging ghost.

I waited until they went past and took off in the opposite direction, running as fast as I could. Of course, that wasn't nearly as fast as the skateboard and hoverboard, and about thirty seconds later, I heard Blake yell, "Hey, slowpoke!"

I glanced over my shoulder. They had done a lap, and now Blake and Santi were headed right for me with

Vladimir in hot pursuit. I pictured him picking me up and tucking me under his arm like a football.

And then I realized that to my left was the store where they'd swiped the wheels. The owner was standing out in front with her hands on her hips.

"Free ride's over, folks! Bring them back in!" she yelled angrily.

When Blake and Santi got close, she ran a few steps and lunged, trying to grab them, but Blake was a good rider and dodged her easily.

While she was distracted, I ran into the store, which was called *Wheels R Us*. It had everything from skateboards and Rollerblades to wheelchairs and mobility scooters to folding bikes. I'm actually not too bad at rollerblading, but I didn't have time to lace up a pair, so I grabbed a bike, rolled it toward the front of the store, and climbed on.

"HEY!" yelled the owner as I pedaled past her into the mall.

Then she yelled, "THERE THEY ARE, OFFICERS!"

CHAPTER TWELVE
A Soft Landing

You know how people say time slows down when something crazy happens? Well, this wasn't like that at all. This felt more like video that had been sped up. All that was missing was a soundtrack of silly music.

I came out of the store behind Vladimir, who was behind Blake and Santi, and I would have been able to just turn around and go the other way if there hadn't been two cops behind me. Fortunately, they were mall cops, not real cops, but they were riding Segways and moving pretty fast.

The Segways even had flashing red lights on the handlebars, which I wouldn't have expected.

"Pull over," said one of them through a little loud-speaker, which also surprised me. It reminded me of the time Trent got a speeding ticket on Interstate 80.

Except, unlike Trent, I had no intention of pulling over. Blake started this, so if anyone was going to explain things to the authorities, it was him. I just had to somehow rescue Santi first.

And I had to do it on a bike that was small enough for him to ride. The folding travel bike I'd grabbed had a seat that could be extended for a full-grown adult—I'd seen people riding them back in Oakland—but the seat on this one was so low my knees practically punched me in the chin every time I pushed the pedals. And when I stood up, I towered over the handlebars and felt wobbly and off balance.

But unless I was going to turn myself in to the mall cops, I had to make it work. Crouching on the bike, I managed to speed up until I was just behind Vladimir's massive back.

"On your left!" I yelled, pulling out to pass and just missing a startled shopper, who dropped her bags as Vladimir and I swerved past her on either side.

"Stop running, Dagmar," said Vladimir calmly. "We must leave mall."

"I'll stop when *he* stops," I said, pointing my chin at Blake. "And besides, I'm not running, I'm pedaling."

When we slowed down to get around a group of mall walkers, Blake and Santi increased their lead. Vladimir glanced over his shoulder at the mall cops, who were gaining on us.

"We need lower level," he said.

"I'll get Santi and meet you at the car," I told him. "Do whatever you want with Blake."

He nodded, and spotting an opening, I pedaled until my tires were spinning like hamster wheels. My thighs ached from the effort, but I was right behind Blake. His skateboard appeared to have reached maximum speed.

"*Santi,*" I hissed.

He turned around and looked at me, his eyes wide with excitement.

"Blake's a expert skateboarder," he told me.

"That's great," I said. "But it's time to get off."

"I'm not slowing down," said Blake, without looking back.

"Then I'll catch up, and you can climb onto my back, Santi," I said.

We were nearing the end of the mall's upper level. To keep going, we would have to make a U-turn to the right. If my circus act had any chance of working, I needed a straightaway.

I slalomed around behind them as we made the first turn, and then the second—when I saw Vladimir heading right for us! Anticipating our route, he had taken a shortcut across a bridge.

With the mall cops zooming up behind and Vladimir

in front, I didn't know what to do, and things were moving so fast I didn't have time to think.

I swerved one way, and Blake swerved the other, right into Vladimir's path. When Blake ducked, Vladimir scooped Santi off Blake's back and tucked him under one arm . . . like a football.

I had amazing powers of prognostication (*foretelling from signs*).

Then, while I coasted and craned my neck to see what happened next, Vladimir had a head-on collision with a mall cop. The cop never had a chance. The bodyguard's massive size, plus the little bit added on by Santi, was too much for even a fully grown cop on a Segway, and he was knocked aside like a ninepin.

The other cop braked to a halt, checked on her partner, and then did a one-eighty after Vladimir and Santi.

Blake and I were going the same direction, but there was a limit to how far you could go in any direction on the second floor, because there weren't any exits. We were either going to have to keep doing loops and figure eights on the mezzanines and bridges, or we were going to have to head for an elevator or an escalator.

On the opposite mezzanine, Vladimir's hoverboard seemed to be running out of juice. The only way he was able to avoid the mall cop was by taking extreme evasive action and swerving in and out of shoppers, half of whom now had their phones out to record the chaos.

One teenager was taking a selfie video and must have been saying something like "check out what's happening behind me" when Vladimir and Santi clipped his arm and sent the phone flying over a railing.

"Blake, forget about escaping from Vladimir," I yelled. "We have to get out of here before we end up on YouTube!"

"So you want to give up?" he yelled back, grabbing a soda out of a startled man's hand and taking a sip before throwing the cup in the trash, all while still comfortably riding his skateboard.

I could not believe he was being such a moron. "No! I do not give up! But I'm canceling your stupid challenge!"

"It's not over until I say it's over," he said with a shrug. "If you want to quit, be my guest."

I was so mad that the next sound I made started deep in my chest and escaped my mouth before I even realized what I was doing. I guess you'd call it a roar of frustration. I would have been super embarrassed if Blake hadn't looked so freaked out.

"RRRRRRAAAAAAAAAAARRRRGGGHHH!" I bellowed, my head feeling volcanic all over again.

And then I knew exactly what to do.

I was nearing the top of the escalators, and Vladimir and Santi were still a hundred yards away. As Blake rolled deeper into the mall, I pedaled for the escalators as hard as I could.

When I was almost there, a stroller appeared out of nowhere, pushed by a mom who seemed to be having a loud conversation with herself but was actually facetiming with someone on a handlebar-mounted phone.

The only way to avoid flattening her and her baby was to crash, so that's what I did, steering into a large planter that stopped my bike and sent me flying over the handlebars. As I skidded to a halt, I looked up and saw a furry head peek out of the stroller—her "baby" was a dog. It was even wearing a pink bow.

But I didn't have time to be mad about that. Climbing to my feet, I staggered to the top of the escalator and looked down. Vladimir and Santi were headed my direction with one Segway-riding mall cop in hot pursuit. The other one had somehow climbed back on *his* Segway and was gliding toward me from the opposite side.

I looked down. As usual, the escalators had a tempting, shiny metal slide between them. Also as usual, the slide was studded with raised metal discs every six feet to discourage daredevils from trying it.

But I needed to get down. Fast.

Swiping a stack of napkins from a nearby table, I hopped up on the slide between the escalators and kneeled, putting a half stack of napkins under each of my bare knees.

Then I pushed off.

My first thought was *I can't believe how stupid I am.*

My second thought, as I watched the raised metal antisliding devices whizzing between my knees, was *This is actually super fun.*

My third thought was *How do I get off at the bottom?*

I flew down the slide, ignoring the startled shoppers riding up (and high-fiving one kid who saw me coming), the napkins making my knees slide fast even as they started to shred (the napkins, not my knees).

"Dagmar!" yelled Santi from above when he saw me.

I didn't know if he was warning me, cheering me on, or simply identifying me for the authorities, but if he saw what I was doing, that meant Vladimir did, too.

I never did decide how to get off the slide—really, my only option seemed to be a face-plant that was going to give me full-body road rash—but fortunately, an eight-foot-tall bunny was shuffling past.

I blinked, thinking I had to be seeing things, and then I was launched off the bottom of the escalator into the well-padded bunny, which must have been on its way to entertain some toddlers. I have no idea if the person wearing the suit was seventeen or seventy, but I heard an "OOOF!" when I shot into them like a missile.

There was no time to apologize or thank the bunny for breaking my fall. Climbing over the fallen furry, I got up as fast as I could and yelled, "Vladimir!"

But he was way ahead of me: Santi was already coming down the slide.

Unfortunately for him, he didn't have the whole napkins-on-knees thing worked out and was bumping his butt every six feet.

"D-D-D-DAG-m-m-m-MAR!" he yelped, trying to slow himself down with the soles of his shoes.

When I helped him off at the bottom, he rubbed his butt and started walking bowlegged, like a cowboy who'd been riding a really bony horse. We started trotting toward the exit as, above us, Vladimir abandoned his hoverboard and ran from the mall cops on foot.

So Santi and I had escaped.

But how were we going to get home?

CHAPTER THIRTEEN
Blake Loses

People pointed and laughed as we moved away from the bunny, who was sitting up woozily. I pulled Santi along until we were camouflaged by a crowd of shoppers who had no idea what was happening. While we hurried toward the doors leading outside, I weighed our options. There weren't many. We could:

A) turn ourselves in to the mall authorities and see what life was like in the mall jail,

B) find our way back to the car and hope Vladimir and Blake escaped and showed up, or

C) try to hitchhike back to the compound.

I ruled out A because even though Trent always told me there was no shame in getting caught by security guards, there was no benefit to surrendering. The big problem with C was that I wasn't sure I even knew how to get back. And I couldn't call Trent because even though I had cell reception, he didn't get it out in the woods.

That left B, which wasn't much of a plan. If the mall cops called in reinforcements, Vladimir and Blake would be surrounded, and we'd be out of a ride.

"Hurry up, Santi," I said.

"My bottom hurts when I walk," he said.

"Well, I hope your skateboard ride was worth it," I told him.

That took his mind off his butt, at least. A huge smile spread across his face.

"Blake's a expert skateboarder," he reminded me.

That was just perfect: now Santi worshipped Blake. What did he *see* in that guy? Besides the expert skateboarding, I mean.

The exit doors were finally in sight. Another set of escalators was coming up, too. And judging from the way people were running and trying to get *off* the escalators, something was happening.

First, I saw a mall cop running down the up escalator. She wasn't making much progress, but I guessed she was trying to avoid the crowd on the other side, which was panicking because BLAKE WAS RIDING DOWN IT ON HIS SKATEBOARD.

Like a surfer, he had his arms out and knees bent to keep his balance while he did a rail slide down the shiny black handrail. As he passed, people leaned back, ducked, or crouched to avoid him, and the chorus of gasps and screams rose like a wave.

"I . . . AM . . . AWESOME!" he yelled.

Who even *thinks* that, never mind yells it?

"He *is* awesome, Dagmar!" said Santi excitedly. "He is *awesome*."

Then he said, "Ow! Quit it!" when I yanked his arm to get him to stop gawking and hurry up.

We reached the bottom of the escalator at the same time Blake did, and I have to admit I was kind of impressed by the way he landed the trick and swerved the skateboard to a stop instead of just falling off the way I would have.

Of course, as soon as he opened his mouth, he was annoying again.

"Did Vladimir catch you yet?" he taunted us.

"Obviously not," I said, "because he's not here."

"Well, he could have caught you and let you go, like he caught Santi. Santi, you're out, and either Dagmar or I will win, except it's going to be me, because I'm the best at this game and I always win."

I was thinking, *How often do you play?* when Vladimir climbed out from behind some shrubbery, wrapped Blake in a bear hug, and lifted him off the ground.

"You are caught," he said. "Now we go."

I could have cheered.

Actually, I think I did.

• • •

WE MADE IT to the car without anything else happening, and a few minutes later, we were on the road.

"How did you get down from the upper level, Vladimir?" I wanted to know.

"I am repelled," he said.

I was repelled by Blake, too, but I figured he meant something else.

"You rappelled?" I echoed. "With what?"

Vladimir looked at me in the rearview mirror, and I could have sworn he winked. "I have manny secrets," he said.

Blake, meanwhile, was grumpy because he'd lost—at least, that's how he saw it. Since I'd canceled his game, I didn't necessarily see myself as the winner, although I was satisfied that he'd been caught before me. Then again, Vladimir could have caught me first, instead of Blake, so . . . maybe he wanted Blake to lose, too. I couldn't blame him. Working for Blake's family seemed like a pain in the rear.

Santi was bummed out, too. All the stuff he'd bought

was gone. Vladimir had dumped the bags because there was no way he could carry them and chase us at the same time. Blake didn't even notice anything was missing and seemed surprised when Santi started crying about losing his junk.

"You can just buy more," he told Santi as if that were the most obvious thing in the world, completely ignoring the fact that we actually couldn't. I still had about a hundred and eighty dollars of his money in my pocket, but I figured I should hang on to it in case we needed it for groceries or something.

"What is *wrong* with you?" I asked Blake, the words coming out before I knew what I was saying.

He had already started playing the shooting game with Santi on the built-in screen, so when he looked up, it only lasted half a second.

"What do you mean?" he asked.

Everything, I wanted to say. He was a rich, spoiled jerk who had no idea how normal people lived their lives. He thought it was funny to create pandemonium (*a wild uproar of anger or excitement in a crowd of people*) and then just walk away like it was no big deal. And he'd gotten us involved without letting us know what we were getting into.

"I just don't know why you have to play that stupid game or why you chose us to play with you," I said.

This time he looked at me—really looked at me. He stopped playing, and his character in the game died while Santi's floundered on. For the first time, Blake looked truly puzzled.

"I invited you because I thought you liked escaping, too," he said.

I didn't know how to answer that. Because he was right. It gave me a weird, shivery feeling to think that Blake, of all people, actually knew something about me.

"Well, I guess you'll be in trouble now," I said as he went back to his game.

He pressed a button on his controller to respawn. "Hasn't happened yet."

As we got closer to the compound, I stopped being mad at Blake and started worrying what Trent and Leya would do when Santi told them what had happened at the mall. They definitely weren't going to let me hang out with Blake anymore, and I hadn't decided if that was what I wanted or not.

They wouldn't let Santi see him, either—which was the leverage I needed.

"Santi," I said, after his character died for the thirty-fifth time. "You can't tell your mom and Trent about what happened."

"Why not?" he asked.

"Because we'll get in trouble," I said.

"Okay, I won't tell," he said. "Unless I forget."

"Well, you can't forget," I told him. "Because if you do, and you tell them, you're not going to be able to see Blake anymore."

His eyes got wide. "Really?"

I nodded. "Really."

Blake must have been paying attention, because he said, "Santi? Do you want a soda before you get home?"

"What kind?" Santi asked.

"Any kind you want."

Santi nodded his head up and down so hard I thought he'd sprain his neck. He had recovered from eating his way around the world and knew that once we got back to the compound, sugar was going to be harder to find than a cell-phone signal.

I imagined Blake was going to press a button and reveal a hidden refrigerator stocked with ice-cold drinks, but instead he told Vladimir to pull over at the little store down the road.

We all went inside, and Santi picked out the biggest bottle of root beer he could find. He chugged half of it in the parking lot, and then the rest of it in the car. As we bumped and bounced up the dirt road, I pictured all that root beer sloshing and fizzing in his stomach.

"Let me see your phone," said Blake, probably

because he wanted to make fun of it for being old and outdated or something.

I honestly didn't care, so I pulled it out of my pocket—and he snatched it out of my hand. Before I could get it back, he turned away and started tapping away with his thumbs.

"Now you have my number," he said, letting me have the phone again. "Just in case you want to hang out again."

I put the phone back in my pocket, thinking I could always delete the number if I wanted to, and that it didn't matter anyway since we didn't get reception.

A little while later, Blake and Vladimir dropped us off, and we walked down the hill. Trent and Leya were excited to see us, and Leya scooped Santi up in a big hug.

"Welcome back! How did it go?" she asked after she put him down.

Santi looked uncomfortable, like ferrets were wrestling inside him. Glancing from my face to Trent's to Leya's, he opened his mouth, and the mother of all burps echoed from deep within his belly: "FIIIIIIIIIINNNNNNNE."

• • •

Trent asked me if I wanted to help him work on the wall. I didn't have anything better to do, and helping him didn't violate my sabotage policy, so I said sure. It was now about twenty feet long and four feet high.

"I think I'm going to turn a corner," he said, showing me which way he planned to go.

"Are you going to build it all the way around the compound?" I asked as I followed him down to the end where he'd left off.

He smiled and shook his head. "I think that would make me feel claustrophobic."

"Why are you working so hard on this, anyway? I mean, when we go, you'll just have to leave it behind, and then all your work will be for nothing."

"Dagmar, you really know how to cheer a guy up." He scratched his beard, then picked up a rock and tossed it from hand to hand. "There are two parts to work: the work itself and the reward you get from it. Some people just work so they can get money and buy things, and the work itself may not be anything they enjoy. Other people find satisfaction in the task itself."

He handed me the rock, and I looked at the wall, trying to figure out where to put it.

"Like piling rocks on top of each other," I said.

"I like making things," he said, guiding my hands to a place where the rock fit perfectly. "Some people just like to keep busy, but I like solving problems, fixing something broken or making something out of nothing. Maybe someday someone will come along and admire this nice wall and wonder who built it."

"But you'll never know," I said, feeling bothered that he wouldn't get credit.

"Imagining it is enough for me," he said.

Building a wall was a lot more work than I'd realized. The biggest part of the job was wandering all over the place looking for rocks and then carrying them back. After a couple hours of that, my back was sore, and my hands were raw and scraped. But it was cool to see how you could make something so strong without using anything to hold it together. It was relaxing, too. We didn't talk much except to tell each other where good rocks were or to discuss which rock went where. And when we took a break and drank cool water out of the pump, it tasted even better than the soda I'd had at the mall.

By the time we quit for the day, we'd turned the corner and added a good two feet to the wall.

"Nice work, Dagmar," said Trent, squeezing my shoulder.

"Good job, Trent," I said.

■ ■ ■

THAT NIGHT, AS I lay in my sleeping bag and watched the star lantern slowly turning, I remembered something Trent and Kristen used to argue about.

Hard work is its own reward, he would say.

Money is the reward for hard work, she'd say. *Hard work alone doesn't pay the rent.*

Weren't they both right? Trent's wall was really cool, and Leya's art installation was getting more and more interesting, but neither of them seemed to be figuring out what to do next. It was like we were stuck in neutral, just coasting along and waiting for someone to come and push us.

Behind Helen Wheels, the little generator putted along, powering the fridge and a light bulb as Trent and Leya stayed up and read books. Finally, the light went out, and I saw Trent's silhouette as he came out of the tiny house and followed the extension cord to the generator. He flicked a switch to turn it off, and all of a sudden I could hear the night: croaking frogs, chirping crickets, the slow trickle of the muddy creek, even the flutter of a moth that brushed past my cheek on its way to the lantern.

Trent paused on the steps and looked at me. I kept my eyes mostly closed so he wouldn't be able to tell I was awake.

After he went in, I waited until I was sure he and Leya were asleep before getting out of my sleeping bag and tiptoeing over to the generator. I'd seen generators before, and I knew how they worked, so it was easy to find the spark plug cap and pull it off. And because I'd planned ahead and hidden Trent's socket wrench nearby, it was no problem to get the spark plug out.

People who don't work with small engines have no idea how important spark plugs are; if there's anything wrong with them, your engine won't run well. And if you get them oily or dirty or bend the ground electrode, they might not work at all.

Usually, a running engine helps you move. In this particular instance, I hoped stopping it would make us go.

CHAPTER FOURTEEN
I Win

In the morning, Trent made huevos rancheros: eggs and beans on tortillas, topped with cheese, salsa, and of course avocado. I guess you could say they're like unrolled burritos, because if you did roll them up, you'd have one heck of a breakfast burrito.

I was hanging bedding on the line afterward when I heard Trent say, "I'd better start the generator. I was enjoying the peace and quiet, but I don't want that food to spoil."

I pretended I didn't hear him. I just kept pinning sheets to the clothesline while he pulled the cord to start the little engine. He tried it again and again, but it just wouldn't start.

He was still tinkering with it while I got the bucket and the watering can and headed off to the pump to pretend to water the garden. When I got back, he was holding the spark plug between his thumb and forefinger, turning it this way and that to see if he could figure out what was wrong.

Finally, he said, "Well, I guess I need to go to the hardware store. Anyone want to go with me?"

"I'll go," said Leya. "If we can find a Salvation Army nearby, I need a few things."

"I'll go if we can get ice cream," said Santi.

"No ice cream," said Leya sternly. "Maybe you should stay here with Dagmar."

I gave Trent a pleading look that said, *I don't want to babysit.*

He understood what I was telling him and said, "Come with us, Santi. We'll get you some other treat."

It gave me a funny feeling to make Trent deal with the engine and Santi when he was being so nice to me, but the way I saw it, he would be better off back in Oakland, too. He needed to be doing real work that helped solve real problems for people—even if it just meant fixing their toilets—instead of building a wall in the middle of nowhere.

Even though the wall was kind of cool.

I wasn't all that surprised when Blake's dogs came loping into the compound half an hour later, snuffling the ground until they got to where I was reading in the shade.

They just stood there staring at me, like they'd done their job by finding me and weren't sure what to do next.

I wasn't too afraid of them, but I didn't reach out to pet them, either: they could chomp my arm up to my elbow in a single bite.

When Blake showed up, I asked, "So what are their names, anyway?"

"Alpha and Beta."

"Seriously?"

"When we got them, my dad watched them play until he figured out which one was dominant and then named her Alpha. Mom asked what we should call the other one, and he said, 'Beta, obviously.'"

"Are they trained to be guard dogs?"

Blake nodded and walked closer. He reached out, put his hand on my shoulder, and said, "Friend, Alpha. Friend, Beta."

The next thing I knew, the dogs attacked—with their tongues. Like puppies that weighed more than I did, they slurped my face, nuzzled me with their wet noses, and generally frolicked all over me until I scrambled to my feet and told Blake to make them stop.

"Maybe we should make it so they don't trust me again," I said.

"Too late," Blake said. "The only way I can reverse

it is to call you an *e-n-e-m-y*, but then they'd attack you with their teeth."

I was glad Alpha and Beta didn't know how to spell.

"Want to hang out?" he asked.

"Doing what?"

"I don't know. We could mess around in the forest, I guess."

If he had said, *Let's go to the mall,* then I would have opened my book and ignored him. There was no way I was going back there. But going to the woods seemed safe enough, since he obviously knew his way around and there weren't any mall cops to chase us.

I closed my book and stood up. "Where's Vladimir?"

"He's back at the house. He can keep an eye on me through the cameras."

Well, *that* didn't feel creepy at all.

I followed Blake down to the creek, but instead of crossing on the plank that had been laid down across the muddy trickle, he led me over to the widest part.

"Dare you to go over on the rocks," he said.

There were enough rocks to make it all the way across, but they were spaced far apart, and some of them were covered with wet, slippery-looking moss.

"I dare you back," I said, wanting to see if he could make it before I tried.

While Alpha and Beta splatted straight through the mud, Blake hopped from one rock to the next and made it across easily. His sneakers were completely dry while the dogs looked like they were wearing black socks.

"Your turn," Blake said.

The first two steps were easy, but I had to stretch a long way to make the third, and when I put my foot down, I was already off balance.

SPLUNK!

I ended up with my left foot on the rock and my right foot ankle-deep in mud.

"I win," said Blake.

I made it the rest of the way without messing up again, and when I reached land, I had one dry foot and one that was soaking wet and completely caked in mud. Blake didn't say *Sorry,* or *That stinks,* or anything. He just turned and headed toward the forest while I followed behind, squelching with every other step and fantasizing about making him eat mud pies.

We didn't have to climb the fence because a little farther away, there was a gate. I hadn't seen it before, obviously, and even if I had seen it, I still would have had to climb the fence because it was locked with a keypad entry system. Blake entered the code while I watched over his shoulder and saw that it was 3-6-7-1-9-9, a number I repeated over and over in my head until I had it memorized.

"Why does your family live way out here?" I asked as we walked through the gate. "It seems like you would live in San Francisco or something, where most of the rich people live."

"My dad says all the best ideas come from nature."

"Even though his inventions have to do with technology?"

"He says tech people can learn from the natural world because everything is connected. Plants and animals communicate better than we can with email and texting. Did you know some kinds of grasses tell microbes in the soil when they need more nutrients?"

I shook my head, even though I was behind him and he couldn't see me. I had no idea how that could possibly work.

"If he's so into being connected and communicating, it seems weird that he barely talks to his brother and sister," I said.

Blake said something I couldn't quite hear. It sounded like, "My family is so messed up. I wish someone would do something."

"What?" I asked.

"Race you to that tree," he said.

It took a while to figure out which tree he meant, because we were surrounded by trees, but once we agreed on the tree and the starting line, I said, "Ready . . . set . . . go!" and started running.

I'm pretty sure Blake started running between "set" and "go," but it probably wouldn't have mattered anyway. I couldn't run very fast because the forest floor had so many obstacles that I had to concentrate on not tripping. We reached the tree in this order: Alpha, Beta, Blake, me.

"I win again," said Blake.

"Alpha won," I pointed out.

He looked annoyed. "Dogs have four legs. Of *course* they beat humans. But I'm the human winner."

And then, as he turned and walked deeper into the forest, I realized something: Blake was trying to make friends. For him, it was like each dare or challenge was a test to see if I was good enough. Which was a stupid way to do it, but Blake was a boy, and sometimes boys can be dumb like that.

He was probably just waiting for me to beat him—he obviously didn't count what happened at the mall—and then he'd think we were equals. So what I needed to do was win one of his challenges.

The problem was that I had been trying my hardest, because I don't exactly like losing, either.

"Are you good at climbing trees?" he asked.

Looking around at the massive redwoods, with no branches to climb up and trunks too big to get my arms around, I had no idea how either one of us would pull it off.

"I'm better at fences, fire escapes, ladders, and lampposts."

"How about throwing things?"

"Pretty good."

So we had a throwing contest: sticks, which we threw like javelins; rocks, which we threw like baseballs; giant pine cones, which we threw like footballs; and moss, which didn't throw well at all and basically just cracked us up.

I almost beat him on rocks.

"Dare you to arm wrestle," I said.

"Challenge accepted."

We found a big, old stump that was flat across the top because some long-ago logger had actually cut down one of these beautiful trees. It was so big we couldn't be on opposite sides from each other, so when we faced off, we just used a little part where it stuck out.

Putting our elbows down, we laced the fingers of our right hands together and then gripped left hands so we couldn't use them for extra leverage. By now I knew that Blake liked to start a split second early to get an advantage, so this time I started pushing between "set" and "go"—the result being that we both started at the exact same time.

He pushed my arm back, but before it went very far, I recovered and pushed his arm back, getting it halfway down. Frowning, he gritted his teeth and regained control, and it took all my strength to keep him from slamming my arm down on the stump.

We pushed back and forth, back and forth, until my muscles started to feel rubbery and I could see sweat forming on his forehead.

Then, giving it everything I had, I smoothly pushed his arm down to the stump with a *SMACK!*

"I WON!" I said, really loud because I was so surprised.

But Blake wasn't just a sore winner—he was a sore loser, too. Giving me an angry stare, he called Alpha and Beta to him before turning around and disappearing into the forest.

CHAPTER FIFTEEN
The Not Lumberjack

Blake was better than me at lots of things, especially being a complete and total jerk. What kind of moron can't stand losing just once after winning every other game all day? Maybe the kind of moron who can't accept that he's been beaten by a *girl*.

I would have loved to give him a tour of my turf back home, sneaking through a drainage ditch, shimmying under a fence, and climbing to the roof of an abandoned factory. He wouldn't have been so smug when he heard someone else's scary dogs start barking. But there was zero chance of that happening.

It was another scorching hot day. Even in the forest, where tall trees intercepted most of the sunlight before it hit the ground, it felt as hot and airless as an oven. There hadn't been a cloud, a raindrop, or a breath of cooling wind for as long as I could remember. If I'd been back at the compound, I wouldn't have moved from my shady reading spot until evening. Here, not moving wasn't an option.

But which direction? I had been following Blake, and he hadn't been following a path. I looked up, trying to find the sun, but the endless tree trunks made me feel dizzy and even more disoriented.

"BLAKE, YOU MORON! I DARE YOU TO COME FIND ME!" I yelled.

It was worth a try.

But nothing happened.

Then I remembered there were cameras in the trees and Vladimir was supposed to be keeping an eye on us. Waving my arms, I turned in a slow circle and yelled, "HEY, VLADIMIR! COME GET ME! I'M LOST!"

I hoped I would hear his voice telling me he was on his way, but all I heard was a fly buzzing around my head.

I imagined my image on the screens in Blake's dad's office, a tiny little figure jumping up and down in a tiny little picture. Yelling was probably a waste of time, because most security cameras don't have audio, and Vladimir might have been checking his phone instead of watching the screens. And maybe there weren't any cameras near me, anyway—they couldn't possibly have them in every part of the woods.

I started walking. The forest wasn't that big, I reasoned, so if I kept going straight, eventually I would come to a fence, which I could follow until I found a gate.

But keeping a straight line wasn't easy. Sometimes I had to detour around a pile of rocks, a fallen tree, or a clump of bushes that might have had poison oak in it. The ground was hilly and uneven. And even though every tree is technically unique, let's face it: after a while, they all start to look the same.

Eventually, I found what might have been a path. I started along it, but I couldn't make up my mind about whether it was really a path or just looked like one. Either way, it was easier to walk on than the rest of the forest floor, so I kept going. By that time, I wasn't paying much attention to my surroundings.

Which is probably why I stepped in the trap.

I heard a sound like a whip, and then something tightened around my ankles. There was a loud *BOING*, and then suddenly I was flipped upside down and yanked into the air like I'd been strapped to a rocket.

A second later, I was dangling ten feet above the path.

I twisted and turned and tried to force my feet apart so I could slip out of the noose that held them together. I tried to do extreme sit-ups so I could reach the knotted rope. But it was no use. I was utterly helpless.

UTTERLY: *carried to the utmost point or the highest degree.*

At first, I wondered how long I could survive without food or water. But after only a few more minutes, I wondered how long I could survive hanging upside down. The blood pooling in my cranium was downright uncomfortable, and just as bad, my ankles were itching and there was nothing I could do about it. Maybe I would die of itchy ankles.

Then I heard heavy footsteps crunching through the underbrush. Wiggling my whole body like a porpoise, I turned around and watched as an upside-down man made his way toward me. I recognized him right away. Wearing heavy brown boots, worn blue jeans, and a plaid shirt with rolled-up sleeves, with a bushy beard that would have made a nice nest for a family of birds, it was Blake's uncle, the lumberjack I'd seen arguing with Blake's dad in the forest. But he wasn't carrying an axe— so maybe he wasn't a lumberjack, after all.

As he approached, I thought the look on his face went from sad to happy, but then I realized he was upside down, so it was actually the opposite: happy to sad. I guessed he hadn't caught the person he was hoping to.

"Who are you?" he asked.

"I'm Blake's friend," I said. "Who are *you*?"

"I didn't think Blake had any friends," he said, ignoring my question.

"Now that you mention it, we're ex-friends. We were almost friends until Blake acted like a jerk for the hundredth time. So I suppose you could say we're frenemies . . . or maybe even just regular enemies."

"Sounds complicated," said the Not Lumberjack.

"Let me down now!" I told him.

There was a *snick* sound as he pulled a long, shiny knife out of a sheath on his belt. I tried to gulp, but I was upside down and my mouth was dry, so it didn't work very well. Fortunately, he walked away from me to where the other end of the rope was tied around a peg driven deep into the ground. Grabbing the taut rope with his free hand so I wouldn't hit the ground like a pile driver, he sliced cleanly through the line.

He lowered me slowly until my hair just brushed the ground. Then, while I stood on my head, he walked over and loosened the rope around my ankles so I could somersault back to my feet.

As I dusted myself off, he slipped the big knife back in its sheath, stuck out his hand, and said, "I'm Lyndon."

"I'm Dagmar," I said, shaking his hand. It was rough and callused from hard work, more than Trent's, even, and Trent had the hardest hands I'd ever touched.

"Look, I'm sorry about catching you in that trap," said Lyndon. "Are you okay?"

"I'm fine." Even though my ankles were bruised and sore with rope burn, I didn't want him to think I was a wimp. "Why are there so many traps around here? Is everyone in your family paranoid?"

He squinted off into the distance, like he was really giving it some thought. "Just because you're paranoid, doesn't mean they aren't out to get you. The traps aren't what you think."

I had no idea what he thought I thought, so I asked, "Did you make them?"

He nodded. "Would you like a glass of iced tea?"

"Sure, I guess. And then can you show me how to get out of here?"

"Of course."

He turned and headed off in a direction that seemed to go even deeper into the forest. But I was so turned around, I had no idea where we were going.

Lyndon moved confidently, always putting each foot in exactly the right place, like he belonged in the woods. I tried to follow along and put my feet where he put his, but he was a lot taller than me, and it didn't work very well. So I scrambled along as best I could.

When we passed under a tall rock outcropping that was mossy and damp with seeping water, Lyndon paused to wet his hand and then wiped the moisture on his forehead. I did the same thing, and it felt cool and refreshing. We wound through tightly spaced trees, ducked under an enormous fallen trunk that hadn't quite reached the ground, and sidestepped down a short slope.

Then there was a house in front of us. It was three stories tall but blended into the woods because it was made of huge, rough-cut planks the same color as the trees. Moss grew on the walls and the shingles of the roof. Everything looked just a little too big, like it was a Popsicle-stick house magically enlarged to full size.

But it must have been solidly built, because when we stepped up on the porch, it didn't creak once.

"Wait here," Lyndon said before going inside.

I peeked in the door behind him and saw a floor made of packed dirt. Ferns and mushrooms grew in the corners. The cool, musty air reminded me of a cave, but it gave me a peaceful feeling.

He came out carrying two tin cups. He handed one to me, and I took a sip. Although it was definitely tea, calling it *iced* tea was a stretch because there wasn't any ice. It was room temperature, but at least it wasn't hot.

We sat down on two stumps that passed for chairs.

"The traps aren't designed for people like me, because they're inside the fence," I said.

"No," he agreed. "They're not for people like you. Most people see the signs and turn back."

"So who are they for? Your own family? Blake said you and your siblings are fighting about something."

Lyndon took a deep drink of tea. Some of it dribbled out of the mug into his beard.

"This land has been in our family since the time of the gold rush, back in the nineteenth century," he began. "A long-ago ancestor came to California searching for gold, and when he didn't find any, he made a fortune doing other things. He delivered supplies with a cart, then opened a general store, and eventually owned warehouses and ships that sailed from San Francisco. He bought this land but never touched it—never logged it, never did anything. It stayed in our family all this time, and after my brother, Reynold, made his first billion, he built a mansion right in the middle of it. My sister and I have the other thirds. He offered to build us mansions, too, hoping to keep us quiet. We turned him down."

"Quiet about what?" I asked.

"Quiet about the fact that his inventions are based on our ideas. He's not the only genius in the family."

"Modest much?" I said sarcastically.

"Reynold went to Stanford, I went to MIT, and Penelope went to Harvard," Lyndon said matter-of-factly. "We used to sit around the kitchen table and help Reynold brainstorm ideas for his PhD—he never would have gotten started without us. He used our breakthroughs to start the business that made him rich and famous. Now he's planning to take the company public, selling it off to shareholders, something that will make him a hundred times richer than he is now. Penelope and I will get nothing."

"So that's what you were arguing about in the woods the other day," I said, remembering how mad the three of them were until Blake distracted them with a firecracker—which, now that I thought about it, was probably a really bad idea when everything was so dry.

Lyndon looked at me like he was just realizing I had been there with Blake. "I built the traps to keep Reynold off my land. If he trespasses and gets hurt, I won't cry about it. It's not just that he used our ideas, it's what he used them for. I wish someone could help him realize his products are doing more harm than good. He's creating a world where everything is done for you, without realizing he's making people helpless in the process. I renounce technology, and I renounce my brother."

He set his cup down on the porch with a clank.

"It's time for you to go."

CHAPTER SIXTEEN
Charades

Blake's family was weird. My family was weird, too, obviously. Most of my friends had divorced parents like I did, but none of them had a mom who was in Dubai and a dad who was broke and a stepmom who made really interesting art but, let's face it, was never going to make a living tying torn sheets to tree branches. And none of my friends were rich, but at least they weren't living in a house the size of a cargo van, without cell phone service, internet, cable, or a reliable source of electricity. But even though we argued sometimes, and my little half brother was as annoying as an alarm clock without an off button, at least we didn't try to hurt each other.

Even if we did sometimes spoil each other's food.

After he got all upset and told me it was time to go home, Lyndon walked me back to the fence, opened the gate, and watched while I crossed the pasture. I turned around and waved when I got to the other side, but he just stared at me. He lived in a beautiful place, but he sure didn't seem very happy about it.

When I got back to the compound, everyone was home, but I could hear right away that the generator wasn't running. Ignoring it would have looked suspicious, so I asked Trent what was going on, and he told me the hardware store didn't have the right kind of spark plug and wouldn't be able to get one until tomorrow.

"I checked my email while I was in town," he added. "I guess you talked to your mom?"

"Uh-huh," I admitted.

He sighed and looked over at his wall, like he couldn't wait to start lifting rocks again. "She's pretty upset with me."

"What did she say?" I asked, feeling guilty for tattling but not *too* guilty, since I was upset with Trent.

"I don't want to put you in the middle of it, Dag," he said with a small smile. "I just hope our lawyers don't get involved."

I understood why: Trent's lawyer was a guy with a ponytail who made his own organic yogurt, and Kristen's lawyer probably wore his suit to the beach, just in case he had to sue somebody.

"If they do, where will I live?" I asked.

"Don't worry about that," Trent said. "You're not going anywhere for the time being."

I walked away, thinking he really had no idea what I was worried about.

For dinner, Leya made a feast with the warm, wilted food, since most of it would spoil before Trent could get the generator running.

She was obviously mad, but she tried to make a game out of it, quizzing me and Santi about what we could eat fresh (overripe fruit, limp lettuce) and what would have to be cooked (there was no way I was eating those soggy mushrooms unless they were sautéed). I wished Trent was doing the cooking—he never, ever uses bulgur, quinoa, or spelt—but I can eat almost anything as long as I have sour cream on top. So I played along, because after all, the whole food thing was my fault.

"Dagmar, is something wrong?" Leya asked while we were eating. "You seem awfully quiet."

"I'm fine," I said.

"What did you do while we were gone?" asked Trent.

"Not much," I lied. "Just hung around and read a little bit."

Just had a fight with my frenemy, got caught in a deadly trap, and talked about technology with a Not Lumberjack in his overgrown playhouse, I could have said.

Would Trent and Leya have been more likely to turn

around and head back to the city if they knew about the dangers in the forest? Somehow I doubted it. Even though Lyndon was glum and Trent was cheerful, I could imagine them hitting it off. Before I knew it, they'd be building stuff together.

So all I could really do was continue making life difficult for the people I cared about until they got fed up and took us all back home.

After dinner, we played charades. The definition of the word *charade* is *an empty or deceptive act*, which was something I was pretty familiar with. The definition of charades the game is *getting someone to guess something without using words*. Basically, you pick a clue written on a piece of paper out of a hat (in our case, it was Trent's sweaty baseball cap) and then act it out until everyone else guesses what it is.

Yes, it's a corny old game from a hundred years ago.

But no, we still didn't have internet or TV.

So it was actually really fun. Leya is absolutely the best at getting people to guess her clues—she never loses. Even when the clue she draws is something impossible like *an idea* or *air*, somehow we guess it right away because her expressions and gestures are always perfect.

You might think that Santi would be the worst at charades, but it's actually Trent. He drew one of the easiest clues, *falling down*, and we were guessing things like *clumsy* and *going downstairs* and *chopping down a tree*.

After time ran out, he accused us of guessing wrong on purpose, just so he would have to fall down over and over again. Santi and I were trying our best, but from the sly smile on Leya's face, he might have been right about her.

Santi was almost as bad as Trent, though, because he would get so stuck on how to act it out that he could never get started. We would start laughing, and then he would start laughing, and then there would be this chain reaction of laughter.

When Trent guessed, "Laughing?" that only made Santi laugh harder. In fact, he laughed so hard that tears started running down his cheeks, so I guessed, as a joke, "Crying?"—which turned out to be the right answer!

When it was my turn, I drew *one big happy family*. But we had a rule that you could exchange one prompt if you wanted, so I put that one back. I got *being bored* instead, which seemed easier, except my pantomime of being bored just confused everyone into thinking I hadn't started.

I kept gesturing to let them know I had actually started, and then I sat there looking absolutely, 100 percent bored out of my skull. I thought it would be a slam dunk.

But they never got it.

●●●

THE NEXT MORNING, after Trent drove off to the hardware store to see if the new spark plug had arrived, I went for a long walk down the road. At first, it felt funny because there wasn't a sidewalk, and back home in the city, I definitely wouldn't have walked in the street because if I had, a car would have come along in nothing flat and creamed me.

But here, there was no choice: if I didn't walk in the road, I would have had to wade through weeds and bushes. Fortunately, there was hardly any traffic. The two times cars passed me, I heard them long before they showed up and moved over to the edge of the gravel. The driver of the first car gave me a friendly wave, but the driver of the second car held the wheel and squinted straight ahead like she didn't even see me.

Every few minutes, I checked the bars on my phone. I had charged it before I sabotaged the generator, and the battery was still at 85 percent. It said *NO SERVICE* for what seemed like a couple of miles, but then finally I saw one bar.

I got so excited I practically ran the next hundred yards, but then it said *NO SERVICE* again. I was in a little canyon, which I thought might have been the problem, so I kept walking until I came out of it.

Finally, a half mile or so later, I suddenly had three bars. Right away I started getting notifications from my friends. I left the road, found a shady spot under a tree, and sat down and started reading. Every single message was about Imani's birthday party, which had been the day before. It looked so fun. They watched a movie, went swimming, and then had a cookout on a patio with an amazing view of San Francisco Bay. Olivia's grandfather had a really nice house.

From a video Nevaeh sent, it looked like it was too windy to light the birthday candles on the cake, but everyone laughed about it, and Imani pretended to blow them out anyway. There were even boys there! Imani had invited her cousin and two of his friends, but they looked awkward and uncomfortable. Olivia and Hailey sent some funny pictures of the boys sitting by themselves without talking and wrote, **The life of the party!**

The pictures and texts made me smile even though I felt super sad and lonely. I had to let them know I was still around.

First, I wrote, **Happy birthday again, Imani! Sorry I missed your party!! Nice job, Olivia!!!**

Then I took a picture of my view so they could see where I was sitting and wrote, **Sorry I haven't been texting more! Still trapped in the boonies. I miss you guys.**

I stared at my phone, hoping to see somebody writing back, but there was no answer. That was weird, because my friends didn't have problems with electricity or cell service, and they pretty much had their phones attached to their bodies 24/7.

A minute passed. Then five. Then, finally, after what seemed like eternity, Imani wrote back!

It's so crazy that you're gone, she wrote. **When are you coming back?**

I don't know, I answered.

Will you be at school next year?

I hope so! I'm working on it . . .

Olivia, Hailey, and Nevaeh joined in with their own questions. Most of them I couldn't answer because I had no idea how long we would actually be here.

Instead, I told them how messed up everything was, and how we got our electricity from a generator (I didn't tell them I sabotaged it), and our water from a pump (I didn't mention that we "showered" there, too), and that Leya had planted a garden (I didn't add that I was killing it). I told them there was a forest with giant redwood trees and a mansion in the forest and that I had met the boy who lived inside.

WHO IS HE? everyone wanted to know.

My thumbs paused over the letters. I knew if I told them he was the son of someone famous, they'd get all excited and want to know more details about him, just like Kristen would have. And in a way, that would have made my disappearance more interesting and mysterious to them. But it also felt dumb to try to make myself sound cooler just because I knew someone rich and famous. Trent and Leya always said that was a cheap way to try to make yourself more interesting, and I suppose I thought they were right about that.

So even though I really wanted to, I didn't tell my friends.

Just some kid, I texted. **He can be kind of a jerk sometimes.**

Sounds lame, Olivia texted back.

Super lame, I agreed.

We ran out of stuff to say after that. I told them I'd keep in touch as much as I could but that I never knew when I'd have cell service.

Then Imani sent a text just to me. **I miss you, girl.**

Miss you, too, I told her. **Don't forget about me.**

Never!!! she answered, which I admit made me cry a little.

A pesky horsefly was dive-bombing my head, so finally I got up and moved away. Now what? My friends all had each other to hang out with, and I had . . . Blake.

I did have his number in my phone. He wouldn't text me, because even though I knew they would have Wi-Fi and probably a cell hotspot at the smart mansion, he knew we didn't have cell service at the compound. And I didn't really want to text him, because he wasn't just lame, he was a jerk. But who knew, maybe he acted like a jerk because everyone in his family was so miserable.

Hey, I texted.

Hey, he texted back right away. **Where are you?**

I walked down the road until I got service, I answered.

Oh.

I wasn't really sure what to write next, but a minute later he wrote, **We could hang out if you want.**

What would we do? I replied.

I don't know. Probably nothing.

OK, I answered, because doing nothing with someone else was better than doing it alone.

CHAPTER SEVENTEEN
The Human Pretzel

We met at the creek. Before Blake arrived, I practiced crossing on the rocks and did it five times in a row perfectly, without getting even a fleck of mud on my shoes. But when I challenged him to cross to my side using the rocks instead of the plank, he just shrugged.

"Why don't you come over to this side?" he asked.

"Because I want to see if you can make it across again without getting your shoes wet," I said.

"You already know I can," he said.

"You only did it once."

"And I won," he reminded me.

Behind him, Alpha and Beta sat on their haunches and looked at me like they'd decided they wouldn't cross the creek, either.

"Fine," I said, and instead of using the plank, I crossed on the wet, slimy rocks, hopping from one to another like it was no big deal and I did it all the time. Everything was going perfectly until I took the very last step. My foot started sliding off the rock toward the mud, so I was off balance when I launched myself at the other side—and my left shoe, the one that was still sort of clean, sank into the goo by the bank.

"Fail," said Blake.

As I wiped my shoe on the dry grass, I tried to remember why, exactly, I agreed to hang out with him again.

"I met Lyndon," I said as we went through the pasture toward the forest gate.

"How did that happen?" asked Blake.

"After you ran away, I got caught in one of his traps."

"I didn't run away," he objected.

"You did too. You lost at arm wrestling, and you couldn't stand losing, so you took off and left me."

Blake didn't say anything to that. He punched in the code to unlock the gate, held it open for the dogs, and asked, "What kind of trap?"

"A rope tightened around my ankles and turned me upside down. I just hung there until he came and found me."

Blake snickered.

"Well, don't tell me you've never been caught in one of his traps," I said as we moved into the forest.

"Well, I haven't," he said. But he said it so quickly and so differently from the way he usually talked that I knew he wasn't telling the truth.

"Liar," I said.

"Am not," he insisted, blushing beet red and absolutely proving he was lying.

"What kind was it?" I needled him. "It couldn't have been one of those big log falls, because you would have gotten squashed flat. Was it a rope trap like mine?"

Angry, Blake swatted some fern fronds out of the way and marched down the path.

"You can tell me," I said, hurrying to keep up.

"It was a pit," he muttered, so quietly I could barely hear him. "He had covered it with a blanket and dirt and pine needles and leaves so it looked just like the forest floor. One minute I was walking along, and then all of a sudden, I was underground. The walls of the pit were too high and too smooth for me to climb out. I just had to wait until he showed up a couple hours later."

"That's quite a soliloquy," I said.

SOLILOQUY: a speech (usually in a play) where a character talks to herself.

"I twisted my ankle, too," said Blake bitterly.

He had stopped walking.

I sat down on a fallen log and looked at him, but he wouldn't meet my eyes. Alpha, or maybe it was Beta, nuzzled my ankles with a wet nose while Beta, or possibly Alpha, roamed off in the trees.

"So Lyndon sets traps in his part of the forest to keep everyone out, and you go there anyway?" I asked.

"They used to just be on his land, but now he sets them everywhere. He really hates my dad."

"What about your aunt Penelope? Does he hate her, too?"

"No, he likes her. I've never found any traps around her house. They're both allies against my dad."

Still not looking at me, Blake came over and sat down near me on the log.

"Do you think this is normal—a family all living on the same land and hating each other's guts?" I asked.

"How should I know what's normal? Your family isn't exactly perfect, either."

I decided to ignore that for now. "Have you ever tried to help your dad, your aunt, and your uncle get along again?"

He picked some old bark off the tree and flicked it away. "How exactly would I do that?"

I slid off the log.

"I don't know," I said.

"Do you want to meet my aunt?"

● ● ●

WE HEARD HER house before we saw it. Through the trees came weird moaning sounds that got higher at the end like questions.

At first I thought it was the dogs whining, but they were right next to us, and the sounds were coming from farther away. Then I thought it was someone making random sounds on a cello, like a string quartet was warming up in the woods—but why would a string quartet be warming up in the woods?

We were walking in a new direction, away from both Lyndon's and Blake's, and the sounds were getting louder and downright creepy. The hair on the back of my neck stood up, and I started to wonder if there was something supernatural living in the woods.

"Whale songs," said Blake.

"Whale songs? We're a long way from the ocean," I said.

Then I heard tinkling, delicate chimes all around, like an army of fairies playing miniature triangles. As if to confirm my thoughts about fairies, fragments of rainbows floated and spun, flickering across the tree trunks and occasionally flaring in my eye.

Was Penelope a witch or a fairy godmother?

Finally, I realized the lights were coming from crystals hung in the trees. Suspended by thread and turning in weak currents of air, they caught rays of sunshine and refracted them into little rainbows that scattered and disappeared as fast as dandelion seeds on a puff of wind. It was like the daytime version of my star lantern.

Ahead of us, a little bird landed on a piece of string that had several different crystals hanging from it—then it took off again, making the crystals and their refractions dance.

"Aunt Penelope is very New Age," Blake told me.

A new path, paved with tightly fitted stones, branched off, and we followed it through a constellation of kaleidoscopic light and increasingly loud whale songs to a house that looked like a cottage right out of a storybook. It had a steeply sloping roof, whitewashed walls, and little windows poking out from under the eaves on the second floor. All that was missing was a trail of bread crumbs leading to the front steps.

Blake walked right up to the red-painted door and knocked, but the sound was barely audible over the moans of ocean mammals blasting out the open windows. When nobody answered, he opened the door, and we both went in.

It was bright and cozy inside, nothing like Blake's mansion or Lyndon's plank house. Narrow stairs led up to the second floor, and a small hallway went past them to the back of the cottage. To our right was an open doorway into the living room, where we saw Penelope wearing yoga pants and twisted into a pretzel so complicated it made me wonder if her body was made out of rubber.

Her eyes were closed, and there was a look of absolute serenity on her face. I would have given anything to feel like that myself, as long as it didn't mean contorting my body and cranking whale songs.

"Aunt Penelope!" called Blake, but she didn't hear him.

In fact, I couldn't hear him, either. I could see his mouth form the words, and I knew what he was saying, but the whales on the recording must have been having a whale of a time, because he was drowned out by a deafening cacophony of *OOOOOOOOO* and *AROOOOOOOO* and *EYAAAAAAAAHHHHHH.*

"*AUNT PENELOPE!*" yelled Blake, but he may as well have been in outer space because not a single word got through.

Then the whale music suddenly stopped—it must

have been the end of the recording—just as Blake bellowed, as loud as he could, "AUNT PENELOPE!!!"

Her eyes popped open in surprise, and she tipped over, her limbs still tied in a knot.

"Ow!" she yelped. "Blake, what are you doing here? Ow! Ow! And who—ow!—is this?"

We rushed forward and helped her untie herself. Grimacing, she stood up.

"Why did you barge in on me like that?" she asked, rubbing her right leg. "I think I pulled a muscle."

"We knocked, but you couldn't hear us," I explained. "I'm Dagmar, Blake's . . ." I stopped before I said *friend*.

"Nice to meet you, Dagmar," she said, stepping forward to shake my hand and wincing like something hurt. "I'm Blake's aunt Penelope, although I guess you already know that. I was just doing my midday meditation."

"I'm sorry we interrupted you," I said.

"No need to apologize," she said, seeming so light and open and friendly that I wondered how she could possibly be related to Blake.

"Dagmar wanted to meet you," he told her irritably.

"That's so nice," said Penelope. "But why?"

"She thinks our family is messed up and I should try to help you and Lyndon get along better with Dad," said Blake.

"I never said that!" I protested.

I was feeling a little mixed up from the crystals, the wind chimes, the bellowing whales, and the pretzel-knotted yogi we'd just knocked over with a yell. But I was also starting to wonder if Blake said what he did because it was what *he* actually wanted.

"Well, what *did* you say?" asked Penelope.

And just then the recording started again.

AAAAAAAOOOOOOOOOOOOOOORRRRRRRRR-RRUUUUUUHHHHHH? queried a whale.

Let me turn off the recording, and we'll talk, mouthed Penelope, or something like that.

CHAPTER EIGHTEEN
Licking the Lawn

Penelope powered down her stereo, excused herself, and said she'd bring us something to drink while we talked. I didn't know how she could meditate in that racket, but maybe the volume was so high it just blasted all the thoughts right out of her head. Though if I ever try it, I think I'll use human-created music instead of whale sounds.

After she left, a cat hopped up on the windowsill and let itself in, purring loudly and seeming happy that things were finally quiet again. It had twigs and bark in its fur from playing outside, so I sat down on the couch and groomed it with my fingers. The room was full of natural things: more crystals, beautiful minerals, gnarled driftwood, and even a giant wasps' nest I hoped was unoccupied.

Blake wandered around, inspecting candles, incense burners, and the drawings and paintings that covered nearly every inch of wall space, most of them depicting dramatic landscapes without people or buildings in them.

I heard nails clicking on the floor and thought it was Alpha and Beta, but Blake had left them outside. A dog I didn't recognize came into the room, a brown-and-white mutt with a broad, scarred face and a missing ear. Then I heard tiny claws skitter across the top of a bookshelf and saw a squirrel racing along near the ceiling. As if that wasn't enough, I realized that the fuzzy blanket in a nearby basket wasn't a blanket at all but a sleeping raccoon.

No, not a raccoon. As it stood up and stretched, I saw its body was too lean and its face was too long to be a classic trash panda.

"Coatimundi," explained Blake. "Aunt Penelope loves animals. If you go to the bathroom, watch out for snakes."

"I can hold it," I told him.

"I'm just joking," he said. *"Probably."*

I heard a high-powered whine coming from the back of the house, like a power saw, and wondered why Penelope would be cutting wood while she had visitors. But when she came back in with a tray and three glasses of bright green liquid, I realized she'd been using a juicer.

"Have some wheatgrass juice," she said. "It's very cleansing."

Blake looked at the opaque green drinks and turned an analogous shade of green himself.

ANALOGOUS: *similar or comparable to something else.*

"Ugh," he muttered.

I didn't like wheatgrass juice, either, although Leya made it often enough that I was at least used to the taste, which was like licking a freshly mowed lawn. As I reached for my glass, my arm suddenly seemed longer than usual, and I knocked it right over, making a grassy green puddle on the tray.

"I'm sorry," I told Penelope, wishing for the thousandth time I wasn't so clumsy.

"That's just fine, Dagmar," she said, even though I could tell she was sad to see perfectly good wheatgrass juice go to waste.

"You can have mine!" blurted Blake, happy to have found the perfect excuse not to drink his.

I thanked him as politely as I could, thinking, *You owe me one.*

As Penelope sat down, I drank the juice quickly, which is the only way to do it. The longer you take, the longer your tongue is dragging across that lawn.

The animals crowded around, and you could tell they really loved Penelope. The coatimundi licked her fingers, the dog sat on her feet, and even the squirrel jumped from the top of the bookcase to the back of her chair and snuggled on her shoulder.

"Animals have pure spirits and love unconditionally," she said. "It's we humans who have bad motivations."

"Do you hate Reynold as much as Lyndon does?" I asked. I couldn't imagine this gentle lady being mad at anyone.

She shook her head. "I feel sorry for him. Money— and the lust for it—is the cause of so many of the world's problems."

I looked at Blake because, after all, she was talking about his dad and not some random billionaire. I could tell he didn't exactly agree with her, even if he wasn't going to argue about it.

"But I do want my share of the fortune," she explained. "There are so many animal shelters in need of generous financial gifts."

The cat's fur was looking pretty good, but when I tried to put it down on the floor, it rolled over on its back, grabbed my hand with its front paws, and started licking my fingers. I guess it didn't want me to stop grooming it.

"Dagmar's right. It would be cool if you guys could all be friends again," said Blake, once again giving me credit for something I hadn't actually said.

"That would be nice," agreed Penelope, "but I'm afraid it's too late for that."

"Maybe you just need something to help remind you that you're all in this together," I said.

"All in what together?" asked Blake.

"Everything," I told him. "Everyone's in everything together, especially families."

"But that's exactly the problem," said Penelope, scratching the ruff of the coatimundi's neck and stroking its long, elegant snout. "We *were* in everything together until Reynold decided he wanted it all for himself. Sometimes too much togetherness has a way of making us not like our loved ones."

"I don't know what either of you are talking about," said Blake, standing up and heading toward the rear of the house. "Do you have anything with sugar in it, Aunt Penelope?"

"You're welcome to look," she told him, grinning at me behind his back. She definitely seemed to be on Team Leya when it came to making sure food wasn't any fun.

After he left the room, Penelope and I petted the animals in silence until she said, "Both Lyndon and I sacrificed our own careers to help Reynold on his way. We assumed we would be made partners in his company and allowed to help steer it in a positive direction. But he never let us in—never even gave us credit for our contributions—and once he takes the company public, we'll be cut out forever."

"What if you just got together and talked and tried to start over?" I suggested as the cat climbed off my lap and jumped out the window.

"The last time we did that, we had a big argument, and Reynold accused us of only wanting his money," said Penelope sadly. "I can't imagine Reynold and Lyndon ever seeing eye to eye."

Blake came back from the kitchen, scowling. "There's no soda, and there's no sparkling water. You don't have chips, candy, sugar, or even honey. What is there to eat in this house?"

"Would you like a rice cake?" asked Penelope.

"I'd rather chew Styrofoam," said Blake. "Come on, Dagmar, let's go."

Penelope walked us to the door and watched us go, lifting one leg above her head as she did.

"Come back anytime!" she called.

"Do you think your dad and your aunt and uncle will ever get along?" I asked Blake.

"I doubt it," he said. "I mean, what's in it for my dad?"

"There's nothing wrong with being nice," I said.

"I don't think he has time for that," said Blake.

CHAPTER NINETEEN
Busted

Leya caught me that afternoon.

I was in the bushes behind the compound, feeding the forest. That's how I had come to think of it, anyway. At least once a day, I would fill a bag with seeds, beans, rice, and grain—all of Leya's favorite food groups—and wander away from Helen Wheels, scattering handfuls for rodents, birds, and bugs to find. I hadn't seen any mice, but a few birds had started expecting me, and would hop and peck at a distance while I gave them a free meal. Once I saw a line of big black ants carrying away crumbs of some zucchini bread I had left the day before. It was crazy how they could move something so much bigger than they were—it would be like me lifting Helen Wheels over my head in two hands and carrying it through the trees.

The reason I wasted the food, of course, was to discourage Trent and Leya. And so far it had been working. Leya was already puzzled by her garden's refusal to flourish.

"This is California, Trent," she would say. "Everything grows here. You have to work hard to kill plants!"

Of course, she had no idea how much effort I'd been putting into doing just that.

And when she checked the tubs of dry goods she'd thought would last all summer, she noticed they were emptying out faster than she expected.

"It's like our food is just disappearing!" she lamented.

Sometimes, she gave me accusing looks—not because she knew I was literally throwing it away, but because she thought I was eating more than my share. But even though I truly was hungry all the time, I never wanted seconds of the tempeh, tabbouleh, and tamari-flavored foods she preferred to meat.

If we'd had any meat, I would only have gotten rid of it by eating it—even though I'm sure there were four-legged carnivores who would have appreciated it, too.

Anyway, I was a couple hundred yards away from the compound, scattering handfuls of stolen food, wondering how much longer it would take for Trent and Leya to decide the experiment wasn't working, when I heard a twig snap.

I froze.

"What are you doing?" Leya asked behind me.

It was pretty obvious what I was doing. Caught red-handed, I turned around slowly. One glance at the fire and fury in Leya's eyes was enough to make me look away.

"Feeding mice and stuff?" I said lamely.

She stared at me disconsolately but didn't say anything. She just turned and walked away.

DISCONSOLATE: *without consolation or solace; hopelessly unhappy; inconsolable.*

"Leya, wait," I said, but she was already too far away to hear me.

I stared at the small mound of makeshift granola mix in my hand, then carefully poured it back in the bag. Rolling the top of the bag to close it, I hurried back to the compound, breathing hard, wanting to catch her before she talked to Trent.

But I wasn't watching where I was going. I put my foot down hard on a rock, half on and half off, and twisted my ankle. Yelping in pain, I fell down, landing on my hip and losing my grip on the bag of stolen food. The bag ripped open, most of the food pouring out as if to prove that even when I was trying to do something right, I couldn't help doing everything wrong.

Blinking back tears, I sat up and tried to pick the

seeds and grain out of the grass, but it was hopeless. I folded the torn bag around the little bit that was left and, cradling it like a wounded bird, climbed to my feet. My ankle was sore, and I couldn't put much weight on it, so I limped onward, favoring my good leg and dragging the hurt one behind.

By the time I got back to the compound, Leya and Trent were huddled together by the wall. Leya saw me first. Looking me up and down, she said one last thing to Trent and then angrily stalked away.

Trent turned and looked at me as I hobbled toward him. Now my hip was throbbing, too, but if he even noticed that I was hurt and dirty and starting to cry, he didn't show it. When I got close, he turned back to his wall and lifted a new stone from the pile.

I plopped down in the dirt next to him, groaning with pain. I think my hip almost hurt more than my ankle.

He still hadn't spoken, and his silence was worse than anything he could have said. I wished he would raise his voice and yell at me, just so I could yell back. Not that he'd ever yelled at me—but couldn't he try it now?

Instead, he just concentrated on his rocks and his wall. I could hear tapping and grinding sounds as he tried one rock and then another, and then finally found one that fit the way he wanted.

The longer he was silent, the harder it was for me to

say something. Words were welling up, but none came out—they all felt stuck in my throat, and I couldn't find the way to unstick them.

Finally, Trent said, "You know our family needs that food, right?" and that did it.

Only instead of talking, I started bawling. I'm not the kind of girl who cries a lot. I mean, I understand it's a natural reaction to pain, sadness, and all that stuff, but I'm also proud of the fact that if I hit my thumb with a hammer, I'm more likely to curse like a grown-up than cry like a little kid. So I've never had much practice. When I started crying, it was a whole-body thing that started in my stomach, whooshed through my lungs, and then spurted out my face in the form of snot and tears and hiccups so hard I almost burped. I'm glad Trent was the only one around, because I'm pretty sure I was doing what people call *ugly crying*.

"I'm s-s-SORRY," I gushed. "I know we need the food, but—but—"

I was going to launch into a whole explanation about my plan, and how I was trying to make them want to go home, but with Trent looking at me—and he has this way of looking so calm even when he should be mad—it all just sounded stupid, and I couldn't say it. I could tell Trent was feeling bad about me feeling bad, because his eyes were twitching and getting wet, which only made everything worse. So even though I wanted to defend myself and explain why I had to resort to sabotage, all I could do was what Leya did—turn and walk away.

Well, because of my hip and my ankle, it was more like limping than walking, but I went as quickly as I could. Over my snorts and sniffles, I heard him slide another rock into place on his wall.

Climbing the steps into Helen Wheels, I emptied my torn bag of stolen food onto the kitchen counter and started separating the rice from the beans and the grains from the seeds and all of it from the twigs and pebbles I'd accidentally picked up. When I was done, I scraped each little pile off the counter into my hand and dumped it into the container where it belonged.

Then I went outside and got the watering can and the bucket and carried them to the pump, trying not to put weight on my ankle and my hip, which was impossible. I filled them both to the top and carried them back to Leya's garden, grinding my teeth with every step. The few seedlings that had sprouted were brown and frail and not very healthy-looking. Carefully, I sprinkled them with the watering can until the dirt around them was nice and moist. Then I refilled the can from the bucket and went back and forth over the whole garden until it was wet and brown and damp-smelling.

"Please grow," I said. "Please."

I heard rustling in the bushes and turned around, wiping my nose with the back of my hand and expecting to see Blake with Alpha and Beta and probably Vladimir, too, just to add to my humiliation.

But it was only Santi, standing there staring at me with big, wide eyes. I didn't know if he understood what was happening, but after a moment he started crying, too.

■ ■ ■

THE WEATHER DIDN'T cool off that evening like it usually did. In fact, with a warm, dry wind coming in from the east, it felt like it got even hotter when the sun went down. After a quiet evening where hardly anyone talked—and nobody talked to me—I turned on the star lantern and lay down on top of my sleeping bag because it was too hot to crawl inside. I hoped the spiders would take the night off from web building so I wouldn't wake up inside a sticky cocoon.

The lights stayed on in Helen Wheels for a long time, so I guessed Trent and Leya were having a hard time sleeping, too. Finally, Trent came out to turn off the generator. After he did, I heard his flip-flops smacking his heels as he made his way over to me.

There was a creak of aluminum tubes and nylon webbing as he sat down in one of the ancient lawn chairs. All around us, the wind rattled the dry leaves of bushes and trees, giving me a kind of restless feeling.

"You know what you did was wrong, right?" he finally said.

I nodded, even though I wasn't sure if he could see me. I thought if I said anything I was going to start blubbering all over again. But then I surprised myself, because the feelings I had weren't about being wrong and sorry. I was just mad.

"Well, what you did was wrong, too, Trent—taking me away from my friends and making me live in the middle of nowhere!" I said. "And all because you made bad decisions and you're bad at business, so you can't afford to pay the rent!"

"What are you talking about, Dagmar?" he asked.

"I saw the papers," I told him. "When you guys were punishing me for trapping Santi, I found the folders for our bills and your business."

I had to give him credit: he actually started to sound mad, too. "You shouldn't have been looking there. Those papers are for me and Leya, not for kids."

"Well, why *can't* I see them?" I asked, sitting up. "If it affects the whole family, why would you keep any of it secret? Santi should know, too, even if he doesn't understand it."

"Because I don't think you understand, either,

Dagmar," he said, standing up and moving over to the lantern like it was a campfire. "These are adult matters."

"I'm smart enough to know you spent Kristen's money on a bad business deal instead of using it to pay the bills, which is why we're all living out here instead of back home where we should be."

That got him. When I said it, he flinched with his whole body.

He turned around, but I couldn't see his face because he was still just a dark silhouette. "Life isn't as simple as it seems when you're twelve years old, Dagmar. Sometimes things don't work out the way we want them to."

"Sometimes, or always?" I said, sounding meaner than I meant to. "If you and Kristen could have worked things out, then maybe we'd have a nice house and nice things instead of . . . whatever it is we have now!"

He answered slowly, like he was choosing his words one at a time. "I'm sorry we can't all earn lots of money like your mom. But we all make choices. I chose to be with you. That may not count for much right now, but it's all I've got."

That made me feel bad. It was true. Even if we didn't have any money and we were living in the middle of nowhere and had no chance that things would get better, he had chosen me. And Kristen . . . well, she chose work, I guess.

Suddenly remembering that I still had a hundred and eighty bucks left over from our trip to the mall, I reached into my backpack for the book I'd been reading that day. Even though I'd finished it since then, the bills were still stuck in the middle like a bookmark.

"Here," I said, holding the money out to Trent. "This will help with the food."

"Where did you get it?" he asked, counting it by the light of the star lantern.

"Blake gave it to me when we went to the mall. He didn't want it back."

Trent hesitated, then folded the money and slipped it into his pocket.

"I'll stop sabotaging things," I told him.

"And I'll try to be more open and honest about what's going on—if you promise to listen," he said. "We're not going to be here forever. We're just lying low and regrouping, living cheap while we wait for a better opportunity."

"But what kind of opportunities do we have out here?" I asked.

He didn't have an answer for that.

CHAPTER TWENTY
Reynold

The wind was blowing even harder when I woke up the next morning. I didn't have a single spiderweb on me, probably because the spiders spent the night holding tight to trees and bushes so they wouldn't get blown away. I was, however, covered in a layer of dust and pine needles and decaying bark—the stuff I think of as forest dandruff.

The surging, swirling wind got annoying fast. My hair kept getting in my face, it was hard to hear people when they talked, and when I went to the pump to take my "shower," the water practically went sideways. The hot air dried my hair before I had a chance to brush it, and I'm guessing I looked like a tumbleweed.

I watered the garden—for real, now that I was done with sabotage—and hung the sheets on the clothesline, where they snapped like flags in the breeze. Then I told Trent and Leya I was going for a walk. Leya hardly looked at me, but Trent gave me a hug that I squirmed out of. He never stays mad for long.

My ankle and hip were still sore, but I wasn't limping too much as I headed down the trail toward the creek, crossed on the plank, and made my way to the pasture. I was halfway across when I had the weirdest feeling, like someone was watching me.

I turned left and didn't see anyone. Then I turned right and nearly jumped out of my skin. No more than twenty yards away, a couple dozen ginormous cows were standing there staring at me, their jaws working slowly as they chewed big mouthfuls of grass.

Cows! Where the heck had they come from? They were reddish-brown, mostly, with white faces and white stomachs, and each one looked like it weighed as much as a Smart car. They looked peaceful, but what did I know? I had never seen a cow in the wild before and was afraid if I made one wrong move, they'd trample me.

On the other hand, they were kind of cute. Not the way horses are cute, with their big, dark, liquid eyes, but the cows were shaggy, and . . . I kind of wanted to pet one.

Moving slowly, with my hand outstretched, I took one step after another until I was ten yards away. Then five. The cows shifted uneasily, and then one of them bellowed, *MAAAAAAW*—nothing like the gentle *moo* I'd expected.

I flinched, and the cows took a few nervous steps back. Close up, they were absolutely huge. I had no idea how anyone got hamburgers out of them.

I took one more step, and they started milling around restlessly, making me worry again about getting trampled. I wish I could say the cows and I made friends. But what happened next, if I'm being perfectly honest, is that I turned around and ran away as fast as my ankle would carry me.

I'm no cowgirl.

I went to the gate and let myself in, then headed for Blake's house. I had barely gotten under the big redwoods when I heard something thrashing through the bushes in back of me. Ducking behind a tree, I sneaked a look, expecting a raging brown-and-white cow or a flying log or even two giant dogs to be bearing down on me.

But it was only a stocky, wheezing, five-year-old boy.

"Did you see those cows, Dagmar?" he asked, saying the word *cows* the way you might say *aliens with tentacles*.

"It was hard to miss them," I said. "How did you get in?"

"The gate didn't close all of the way," he informed me.

I must have been too distracted by my bovine encounter to have noticed whether it clicked into place.

"That's fascinating," I told him. "Now go home."

"Why were you throwing away food?" he asked.

"I wasn't throwing it away; I was feeding the forest," I said as I started winding my way through the towering trees, figuring he'd get scared and turn around.

"Forests don't need food," he said, following me.

"There are lots of hungry things in forests," I said. "Big animals that like to eat small kids, for example."

He looked around nervously. "I'm not small! But why do things in forests need *our* food?"

I shook my head. It was as if my guilty conscience had become real and taken the form of a five-year-old boy with boogers under his fingernails.

"You wouldn't understand, and anyway, you don't have to worry about it anymore," I told him.

"Don't you *like* us?" he whined, falling a little farther behind.

That was a question I couldn't answer honestly. I think it's possible to love someone without liking them very much, and that's exactly how I felt about Santi at that moment.

"Go home!" I yelled, maybe a little louder than necessary.

"I might get lost," he said. "Will you go with me?"

I was so annoyed and out of patience that I just yelled as long and loud as I could while Santi covered his ears. When I ran out of breath, I could hear my own voice echoing in the trees.

"I'll wait here until you get back," said Santi in a small, scared voice.

He sat down right where he was and stared at me—until he realized he was sitting on an anthill. Jumping up, he danced around and slapped his legs until he finally got all the ants off. He looked too nervous to sit down again.

As much as I wanted to leave him, I wasn't 100 percent sure I'd remember where he was when I came back later. And I definitely couldn't afford to get blamed for losing him.

"Fine, follow me," I snapped. "But don't talk to me. In fact, don't even think about talking to me. Don't talk, or think, just stay behind me and don't get in the way."

"Okay," he said.

"I said DON'T TALK!"

"Sorry!" he yelped.

Apparently, he couldn't help speaking when spoken to, so I just glowered at him before turning around and marching off. I promised myself I wouldn't turn around to see if he was keeping up.

I caved once, though, and when I did, he gave me a huge smile, like he was so proud of himself he couldn't stand it.

"See?" he said. "I'm not saying anything!"

• • •

REYNOLD BERTHOLD HIMSELF opened the door.

Not with his hands or anything. When I pressed the doorbell, a voice asked, "Yes?" sounding so crystal clear I thought there was someone outside on the porch with us. But it was just the billionaire's surround-sound intercom.

"It's Dagmar," I said.

"And who is that with you?" asked the voice.

"Santi," I said, looking for the hidden camera but not finding it. "We're here to see Blake."

The door glided open to reveal a man in gray slacks and an ironed white shirt. He was standing about ten yards back from the door and holding a tablet, so apparently he did the whole thing by remote. It was pretty cool, but still, I wondered what was so hard about turning a doorknob.

"Are you Mr. B—Blake's dad?" I asked, just to make sure.

He nodded. "Vladimir told me about you."

It was weird to be around someone so famous, even if I hadn't heard of him before Trent and Leya told me who he was. He was short and skinny with furry-caterpillar eyebrows and a shiny bald head that made me think of a turtle. For some reason I'd expected him to be bigger.

But even if he was a billionaire, he put on his underwear one leg at a time just like the rest of us—I knew that because his polka-dot boxer shorts were showing through the fly he'd forgotten to zip all the way up.

Santi must have seen it, too, because he giggled.

But Reynold Berthold didn't notice. He just tapped his tablet, and the door silently closed behind us. Then, frowning at his screen, he padded away in slippers to another part of the house.

"I told Blake you're here," he said over his shoulder just before he disappeared.

While we waited in the entryway, I looked around, noticing things I hadn't seen on my previous visit. There were touchscreens instead of light switches, and I couldn't see a single electrical outlet or even a switch on a lamp. Every cord was hidden, and everything was controlled by voice or touch.

"Lights out," I said, but nothing happened.

"Turn off the lights," said Santi, and suddenly we

were plunged into darkness except for dim sunlight coming through green-tinted windows.

"Turn *on* the lights," I said, and they came back on so brightly it felt like we were caught in the glare of a spotlight.

"Turn off *some* of the lights," said Santi, which worked, except now the lighting made me think of a haunted house in a horror movie. We needed to fix it before Blake showed up.

"Turn on all of the lights and dim some of the lights," I said, just as Blake and Vladimir opened a door and came in. They were wearing matching tracksuits and had white towels draped over their shoulders.

Now the entryway was so dim it looked like twilight.

"Why are you messing with the lights?" asked Blake. Then, without waiting for an answer, he said, "Light setting day number one," and the lights all went back to the way they'd been when we came in.

"Why don't you have light switches, like normal people?" I asked.

He looked surprised. "I told you; it's a smart mansion. Everything is connected so we don't have to run around doing things one at a time. My dad says technology makes it easier to get things exactly the way we want them."

I thought about Helen Wheels with its three light bulbs: one for the living room, one for the kitchen, and one for the sleeping loft. It was easy enough to get things how we wanted with three light switches. And we had our own version of voice-activated control: we just asked whoever was closest to flip the switch.

"It depends on the house," I said.

"Vladimir, you can go," Blake told his manny.

"But you still need elliptical machine," answered Vladimir. "Also free weights."

"I'll do them later," said Blake, sounding snotty. "Leave us alone."

As Vladimir turned to go, Blake took the sweaty towel off his neck and handed it to him. The hulking man didn't change expression. He just took the towel and left.

Money is weird, I thought. It changed the way most people behaved. Vladimir obviously needed the money Blake's family was paying him, or he wouldn't have taken orders from a rude twelve-year-old. And maybe, just maybe, Blake wouldn't have been so rude if his dad didn't have so much money.

It was also entirely possible he was born that way.

"So why are you here?" he asked.

"I thought I'd see if you want to hang out, because I literally don't have anything better to do."

Blake surprised me by grinning. It only lasted a moment, but I guess he thought my insult was a good joke.

"I don't have anything better to do, either," added Santi behind me.

For a moment I thought Blake would laugh, but that would have been a little too far out of character.

"Do you guys like swimming?" he asked instead.

CHAPTER TWENTY-ONE
Smoke

The water in the Bertholds' pool was exactly the right temperature: not too cold, not too warm, just cool and refreshing. There was a hint of chlorine but not so much that it burned my eyes like at the public pool back home. Technically, it wasn't a *natatorium*, which is *an indoor swimming pool*, because it was half inside and half outside, with a retractable glass wall that sealed it off if they didn't like the weather.

In the changing room, we picked out swimsuits from an assortment of different sizes, all brand-new, and grabbed fluffy white towels. There were even goggles and swim caps, but I didn't bother with those because I figured swimming in that nice, clean water was the perfect way to get the dust out of my hair.

The pool looked like something out of a glossy magazine. The furniture around it was real wood, not plastic, and everything on the deck was spotlessly clean. Blake's mom looked like someone out of a glossy magazine, too, when she came out wearing a pretty, flowing print dress and carrying a platter of food.

"Hello, kids, I'm Anjali, Blake's mom," she said. "I brought some snacks in case you get hungry."

I was already hungry, so I climbed right out of the pool to inspect the food. First, I shook Anjali's hand because I wanted to be polite. She wiped hers on a towel afterward, which I'm sure was only because mine was so wet. Anjali was really beautiful, with long black hair and an awesome nose and big brown eyes.

On the tray was a bed of crushed ice, and on the ice was an assortment of oysters, sushi, and sashimi.

"These were all swimming in the Pacific this morning," she said with a smile.

"Except the oysters," I told her.

"No, the oysters, too," she assured me.

"Oysters don't swim," I said. "They drag themselves along with a foot until they find something to hold on to, and then they cling."

She laughed, and I said, "No, really," and then she laughed again, like I was just *so funny*. Her laugh was weird, kind of an *a-ha-ha-ha*.

Blake and Santi didn't bother to get out of the pool.

Blake, pretending to be a submarine, was chasing Santi, who's not a very good swimmer, so he was flailing around in the shallow end.

We don't eat raw seafood in our family, mainly because we can't afford it, and I had never had an oyster in my life. I picked one up and eyeballed it. It looked like a whale booger.

"You just lift the shell to your lips, tilt it back, and take the whole thing in one slurp," said Anjali.

I didn't want her to think I was chicken, so I did what she said and gagged it down. It had the taste and texture of whale snot—salty and clumpy and gross. I swallowed it even though my eyes were watering because I have better manners than to spew half-chewed food all over the table.

"It's good," I lied. Trent told me once that lies are okay if you're lying to be polite.

Santi had climbed out of the pool and was running and shrieking around the deck while Blake swam after him, lying in wait everywhere he tried to get back in. Santi was loving it, and I thought maybe Blake wasn't all bad if he was willing to play with the gnome.

I didn't like the look of the sashimi, but one of the pieces of sushi had cooked shrimp on it, so I gobbled that down. I was just contemplating removing the fish from the rest of the sushi so I could eat the rice when

Santi suddenly cannonballed into the water right next to us and soaked everything: the furniture, me, Anjali, and the seafood platter.

"Oh, dear," she said as the pool water melted the ice and the fish started to float. "I'd better get another one."

"Don't worry about it," I told her. "I'm full anyway."

Then I got a whiff of something that wasn't chlorine, fish, or even the flowery perfume Anjali was wearing.

It reminded me of a campfire.

"Do you smell that?" I asked.

She tilted her head back and sniffed the air. It really was a magnificent nose: not too big, not too little, but interesting enough that you noticed it. I touched my own proboscis and wondered if anyone ever looked at me and thought, *What a beautiful beak!*

"Wood smoke," she said. "I'll bet the cook is heating the wood-fired oven. We're probably having flatbread for lunch, or planked salmon. Does your family have a wood-fired oven?"

"We just have a regular stove," I said. "I wanted to cook hot dogs over a campfire, but Leya says hot dogs are bad for you and Trent says it's too dangerous to light a fire."

"I see," said Anjali, looking puzzled.

She carried the soupy snack platter back inside while I thought about the fact that there was a cook somewhere inside that huge house, working away while we played in the pool. I didn't think about it for long, though, because Santi and Blake were looking the other way, giving me the perfect opportunity to cannonball between them. When I came up for air, they were going in opposite directions, coughing and snorting out the water I'd splashed up their noses.

Direct hit.

We played water tag and Marco Polo and water basketball with a floating hoop Blake dragged into the pool. Meanwhile, the smell of smoke got stronger and stronger, until it seemed like the hot wind was fanning campfires from a Boy Scout Jamboree. If the Bertholds' cook used that much wood to make flatbread, she was going to burn everything to a crisp.

I had a bad feeling, so I climbed out of the pool and toweled off, then walked to the glass railing to see if I could spot anything different. The forest looked normal, but the blue sky had turned gray, and the sun was fading to a pale yellow dot.

"Get out of the pool, Santi," I said. "Something's wrong."

"Just a minute, Dagmar," he whined.

That's when I realized something else was wrong. Santi wasn't moving. He crouched in the shallow end with a look of concentration that could only mean one thing: he was peeing in the pool.

"Santi!" I snapped. "Get out *now*!"

He just shook his head. Blake didn't realize what was happening, but if I couldn't stop the gnome, at least I could rescue our host.

"Blake, come here quick," I said. "Hurry."

He climbed out of the pool just as Santi's look of concentration turned to one of relief. Honestly, you can't take a five-year-old anywhere.

Once we all got dried off, we went through the doors into the main house, where it was so cold I instantly got goose bumps. Reynold, Anjali, Vladimir, and a woman wearing a chef's uniform were all standing in the living room, staring at a screen so large and thin it seemed like a hologram. It was solid, though, because Reynold changed the view by swiping and pinching and rotating his fingers while Alpha and Beta lay on the floor at his feet.

It took me a minute to realize we were looking at an aerial view of the surrounding area. The landscape looked wrinkled, like a piece of paper that had been crumpled and uncrumpled a bunch of times. Some of it was green, but most of it was brown, and in the upper corner, smoke was puffing away like it was coming out of a volcano.

"What's going on?" asked Santi.

"Wildfire," said Reynold.

He sounded calm, but my skin prickled with a cold feeling that had nothing to do with the air-conditioning.

"Should we evacuate?" I asked.

"Don't worry, Dagmar," said Anjali. "Reynold says it's still two ridges over, and the authorities haven't issued any warnings yet."

"But the wind could blow it toward us," I said.

Reynold tapped the screen and brought up a weather report that had so much information it was probably what the TV weather ladies studied before they dumbed it down for the rest of us. He squinted at the numbers and arrows and graphs, and then said, "It keeps shifting. Still too soon to know either way."

I saw the cook and Vladimir look at each other like there was something they wanted to add, but they weren't going to do it.

I went over to the cook and introduced myself. "Hi, I'm Dagmar. Thanks for the, um"—I wasn't going to say *whale boogers*—"treats."

"I'm Summery," she said. "And I know it's an adjective. My parents liked the name Summer, but they wanted to be different."

"I can relate," I told her. "My name means *day maiden* in Old Norse."

"Wait a minute!" interrupted Blake, and we all looked at him. "Does this mean we're not getting flatbread?"

Anjali looked anxious. "Summery told me she was planning to make lobster BLTs and a cold melon soup. How does that sound, Blake?"

"After I heard you say we might be having flatbread, I really started wanting that," said Blake, pouting.

"What do you think, Summery?" asked Anjali.

"Boy, are you spoiled," I told Blake. "What's wrong with a sandwich?"

Something else was bothering me. I went up and stood next to Reynold at the screen. After a minute, I picked out the Bertholds' enormous house, but I still couldn't locate the compound and Helen Wheels.

"Where are my parents on this?" I asked. "Are they in danger?"

Reynold seemed to know more about us than we knew about him—right away he pointed to the place, and I could see the small clearing, Helen Wheels, and Trent's wall, which looked a heck of a lot smaller from miles in the air.

"I wouldn't worry," said Reynold. "They're the farthest away of any of us."

"Who's closest?" asked Blake, suddenly interested.

"Your aunt Penelope," said his dad.

And that's when the power went out.

CHAPTER TWENTY-TWO
The Stupid Mansion

Without power, the house that had seemed so magically alive felt like a tomb. The cracker-thin screen we'd all been staring at became a dull black mirror. Every one of the carefully hidden lights went out, and the ice-cold air stopped flowing out of the vents. In an instant, the room became stuffy and quiet, with only dim green daylight filtering in through the tinted windows.

"I want to go home!" said Santi, sounding scared enough to wet his pants if he hadn't already peed in the pool.

"The fire must have destroyed a transformer," said Reynold matter-of-factly. "The power grid has always been a little bit unstable out here in the country. We'll just wait for the backup generators to come on, and then we'll research our options."

He acted like they would come on at any moment, so we all just stood there waiting—everybody except Blake, who flopped onto a couch with a loud sigh.

But the generators didn't come on. One minute passed, then five, before Reynold said, "Something's wrong."

No duh, I thought.

"I will check generators," said Vladimir, heading quickly out of the room with the dogs loping along behind him.

Anjali and Summery had their phones out, trying to see if they could get a connection, but it was no use. There was no cell service here, either, and without Wi-Fi, the phones weren't any more use than paperweights.

"Reynold, do something," said Anjali in a shaky voice. "Do something *now.*"

"Wait for the power," he said sharply.

"But we don't know how fast the fire is moving," she said.

"You said Penelope was closest to the fire," I reminded him. "Shouldn't we go get her?"

"I don't think it's come to that yet," said Reynold, starting to pace back and forth.

Blake sat up. "Dagmar's right. Aunt Penelope could be in danger."

"Just wait until the power comes back up, and we'll contact her if necessary," said Reynold.

"How far away is she?" I asked.

"About twenty minutes if you're walking," said Blake.

"We can run it in ten," I said.

"Blake! Wait here like your father says," ordered his mom, but to be honest, she didn't sound very convincing.

Blake was off the couch and ready to go. I couldn't tell if he was concerned about Penelope or excited to disobey his parents, but either way, he wasn't going to let them stop him.

"We'll be back soon," he said.

"And you're bringing Penelope here?" asked Reynold. "I haven't given my permission for that."

"It's a rescue, not a social visit, so forget about your family's feud for now," I said.

"That's easy for you to say," he fumed. "Your own flesh and blood aren't plotting against you!"

I just ignored him. What was *with* these people?

I told Santi to wait with the Bertholds because I knew he wouldn't be able to keep up. Then Blake and I ran to the front door, ready to sprint through the forest and warn Penelope.

There was only one problem: the door wouldn't open. It was sealed tight as a bank vault and just as impossible to budge. There wasn't even a handle to pull on—all I could do was smack it with my palms in frustration.

"It's an electronic lock with a power assist," explained Blake. "It won't work with the power out."

Vladimir must have been having problems with the backup generator, because we still hadn't seen even a flicker of electricity.

"What about the other doors?" I asked.

"They all work the same way."

"Can we crawl out a window?"

"They don't open. The whole house is climate controlled."

I wondered if it was possible to suffocate in a sealed house without air-conditioning.

"Smart house, my butt," I said. "This place is STUPID."

"Hey!" said Blake defensively.

Then I remembered a way out. "The pool deck! We can go out the sliding doors and then over the railing."

"It's a long way down," Blake said, sounding doubtful.

"It's either that or stay here and let your aunt fend for herself."

"Let's do it," he said.

When we ran through the living room again, his parents were arguing and Santi was crying, but we didn't even slow down. We ran straight through to the pool area and, after a quick stop in the changing rooms to put on our regular clothes, headed out to the railing.

It was about fifteen feet down to the ground, but I figured if we hung over the railing and then dropped, it was really only ten feet. The hard part was going to be landing on my sore ankle, so I made sure my left foot touched first, then bent both my knees and rolled when I landed. It almost knocked the wind out of me, but I was fine, and Blake did okay, too.

We stood up and brushed ourselves off. The smoke smell was even stronger now, and I wondered if we were about to make a big mistake. Then again, until the power came on, we couldn't get back into the house, so really there was only one way to go: forward.

"Let's move!" I told Blake, and we started running.

■ ■ ■

THE HOT WIND blew in our faces, and the smoke made it hard to breathe without coughing, but we made it there in less than ten minutes. As we reached Penelope's house, the wind chimes were going crazy, and the crystals were bobbing on their lines without any sunlight to reflect. Instead of whale songs, I heard a distant roar that sounded like a passing freight train.

"Aunt Penelope!" called Blake as he yanked open the front door.

There was no answer from inside the house, but the brown-and-white dog with the missing ear came around the corner and whined anxiously. His flat face was scarred like he'd been in a lot of fights, but instead of looking scary, he just looked scared.

"Where is she, Russell?" Blake asked.

Maybe he actually expected the dog to answer or point and bark like a dog in a movie, but Russell just whimpered and whapped his tail on the floor. I stepped forward to scratch his head, and he licked my hand like I'd used meat juice for hand lotion.

In the living room, the cat, the squirrel, and the coatimundi all seemed agitated, and a gray parrot I hadn't noticed before was flapping its wings and squawking. We raced through the house calling Penelope's name, but there was no answer.

I slipped through the kitchen door into the garage, where, instead of a car, there was a large, smooth white thing that looked like a space sarcophagus on the floor. Curious what was inside, I lifted the heavy lid.

And screamed.

Penelope was lying on her back with her eyes closed, still as death.

Before I could decide if she was a New Age vampire

or what, she opened her eyes and, instead of screaming back at me, smiled beatifically.

BEATIFIC: *having a blissful appearance.*

It was while she removed her wireless earbuds that I realized she was wearing a swimsuit and floating in water that smelled like salt and rose petals.

"Hello, Dagmar," she said. "I was meditating in my isolation tank. I'm afraid I lost track of time—I find the sound of crashing waves very soothing."

"Sorry to ruin your relaxation, but you need to get out right away," I told her.

"Do we have plans?" she asked, confused.

Blake crashed into the garage behind me, looking happy and terrified. "Fire, Aunt Penelope! Fire, fire, FIRE!"

"Oh dear," said his aunt, standing up in the tank. With water dripping off her, she looked strong and majestic, like a statue or a sea creature. "Can someone please hand me a towel?"

. . .

SHE MET US in the living room after she had dried off and gotten dressed.

"How much time do we have?" she asked.

"Not much," I said. "The fire is moving fast."

"Come to my house," said Blake.

She frowned. "I don't want to be anywhere I'm not welcome."

"It's not up to you, and it's not up to Reynold," I said. "Blake and I decided."

Blake nodded in agreement.

"You realize it's not just me," said Penelope, opening her arms to include the menagerie crowding around us.

"Trust me, we know," I said.

Apparently she didn't believe in collars or leashes, so it took us precious minutes to find rope for Russell the dog and Carl the coatimundi. I was worried they would panic and run away, so I wanted to make sure they stayed close to us. Yma the bird was shoulder trained, and Farrell the squirrel was happy enough to climb into Penelope's shirt pocket, but that still left Totoro, the cat.

I remembered that, when Santi was a baby, Leya used to make a carrier for him out of a big scarf because we couldn't afford a BabyBjörn. She just folded it in half, tucked him in, and knotted it behind her neck. Grabbing a large piece of fabric off the back of a couch, I showed Penelope what I was thinking, and she coaxed the cat into place and helped me put the whole thing together. The next thing I knew, I had a hot, purring ball of fur snuggled against my chest.

"I guess he likes it," I said.

"Can we go already?" asked Blake, looking out the window at the billows of smoke rolling across the yard.

With Penelope carrying Yma and Farrell and leading Carl, and Blake holding Russell's leash—and me with Totoro in the sling—we left the house.

The smoke was getting so heavy that, even though it was still early afternoon, it seemed like dusk was falling. We still couldn't see a single spark or flame, but over the moaning of the wind, we could hear an eerie crackling sound. A plane flew high overhead, completely invisible.

"I hope your house is going to be okay," I said, panting as we made our way forward. "Maybe the wind will change direction and firefighters will stop the fire."

"I hope so, too," said Penelope. "Everything I own is in that house."

Yma gave a loud squawk and pecked her on the head. It must have hurt, but Penelope just smiled.

I turned around to take one last look at the house.

Then I squawked, too.

Behind the cottage was a towering orange wall that reached to the treetops and gave off a light like a setting sun. Penelope's house looked small and completely doomed.

She and Blake turned around, too.

"Fortunately, everything I *need* is between my ears," said Penelope grimly.

"Not for long if we don't run," said Blake, holding tight to the leash as Russell took the lead.

With the fire bearing down on us, none of us needed any more encouragement.

We ran.

CHAPTER TWENTY-THREE
Rescued?

Sometimes in a dream, I run as fast as I can but hardly move. If I'm being chased through a forest by monsters, for example, it's like I'm running in place while they zoom up behind me.

This wasn't like that at all. I ran as fast as I'd ever run in my life, and for once I didn't slip, stumble, or fall. Fear of being burned to a crisp is a powerful motivator.

By the time we reached Blake's house, we could see fire on three sides of us—it was spreading and picking up speed.

Blake put his thumb on a flat black panel next to the doorbell.

"I hope it opens, because I don't know how we'll all get up the side of the pool deck," he said, coughing.

The door started to open—and then stopped. We

squeezed through the foot-wide opening one by one and heard Reynold cursing loudly. I guess he wasn't always as calm as he looked.

As we went into the living room, the power came back on again, and the whole house went haywire: the windows changed tints, screens went up and down, and every single light in the house came on to a cacophony of beeps and boops and other alerts.

"What's going on?" asked Penelope.

Her brother Reynold glared at her but addressed the rest of us as though she wasn't even in the room. "There's a problem with the generator. Vladimir can't keep it going, and every time it comes back on, the whole house reboots!"

Russell was barking at a hologram of a flickering fire in the fireplace, Farrell was chattering at a robotic vacuum cleaner, and Yma was squawking loudly as a small drone circled the room for some reason.

"Did you have to bring these ridiculous animals?" thundered Reynold.

"Still waiting for a heart transplant, I see," said Penelope. "If you kick them out, you'll have to kick me out, too."

Reynold threw up his hands in disgust just as Alpha and Beta raced around the corner on clicking toenails, drawn by the sound of Russell's barking. Carl slunk between my legs, tangling me in his leash and nearly making me flatten a still-purring Totoro.

"Alpha! Beta! Stop!" yelled Blake as the bigger dogs pounced on Russell, who meekly flopped onto his back and offered his belly.

Fortunately, after some sniffing and barking, the mastiffs decided they weren't going to eat the intruder—they were going to play with him. All three dogs began bounding around the room and knocking things over.

Vladimir came out of the basement, wiping his hands on an oily rag. His face was smudged and dirty.

"Generator is working, but I don't know for how long. We must leave soon."

"What are we waiting for?" asked Blake. "Let's get in the cars and GO."

Vladimir shook his head. "Road is impossible."

"I think he means it's *impassable*," I clarified.

The big manny nodded. "Yes, impossible. It goes into fire, and trees fall across. We saw on screen when you were gone."

Reynold was now in another room, yelling into a phone that apparently worked over the internet. The woofing dogs had moved off to another part of the house, making it easier to hear.

"Your father is speaking with the helicopter pilot," said Anjali. "It will be here soon."

Summery crouched down to pet Carl, who kept winding his leash around my legs. "Will there be room for everyone?" she asked.

"I'm sure there will," said Anjali. "Reynold always orders the best. He'll certainly ask for the largest helicopter available."

"But what about Lyndon?" I asked, just as Reynold came back into the room and ended his call.

"Lyndon turned his back on all technology," he said. "The man wouldn't climb into a helicopter to save his own life."

"He turned his back on you," said Penelope, "because you turned your back on him, and because of what you represent. If you asked him, I think he would come."

"I'm not asking him anything," said Reynold with finality.

"You guys are unbelievable," I said. "Blake, can we at least find Lyndon on the surveillance system to see if he's okay?"

Blake shook his head. "There aren't any cameras on his land."

Out of the corner of my eye, I saw Vladimir and Reynold exchange a guilty look.

"Wait a minute," I said, walking right up to Reynold as Totoro wriggled his head out of the scarf and looked at him, too. "*Are* there cameras on his land?"

Reynold Berthold the billionaire looked like someone had slipped an ice cube down the back of his shirt. "Well, there's one. It's not like I spy on him or anything—"

"HA!" said Penelope.

"But I just wanted to make sure, you know, he wasn't trespassing on my land, or doing anything, you know, dangerous."

"Argue about it later," I said, racing for the office. "We need to find him now."

The screens were up, and the cameras were working, although most of them were blinded by smoke. Reynold reluctantly showed us how to access the secret camera, which was high on a tree and aimed directly at Lyndon's wooden house. We couldn't see him at first, so Blake grabbed a joystick and started panning the camera left and right and up and down.

Finally we saw him. He was up on the roof, using a block and tackle to raise a rain barrel up to the very top. His muscles strained as he pulled on the rope, but the barrel was nearly there.

"He's trying to soak the shingles so sparks don't set the roof on fire," I said.

"See? He's very resourceful," said Reynold. "He'll be fine."

Even though the barrel must have held fifty gallons of water, I didn't see how Lyndon could slow the raging fire for more than a moment.

Penelope obviously agreed. "It's never going to work," she said. "We need to take him with us."

"Impossible," said Reynold. "The helicopter will be here any moment, and so will the fire. There's no time."

As I was calculating whether we could make it to Lyndon's house and back, the power went out again. Every screen in the room went dark.

"This house needs new batteries," said Santi.

Reynold Berthold glared at him.

"Or maybe it needs to work without electricity altogether," I added.

"Will you rebuild if it burns down, Reynold?" asked Anjali. "I don't want to be homeless."

"We have other houses, Mom," Blake reminded her.

"We should get ready for helicopter," said Vladimir.

"Good idea," said Summery before asking Penelope, "Can I carry your coati?" She had obviously taken a liking to Carl.

We trooped out of the office to the front door, which had again sealed tight as a vault during the house's latest reboot. Even the muscle-bound Vladimir couldn't get it to budge.

"Looks like we'd better wait by the pool," I said, hoping the helicopter had a rescue basket or at least a rope ladder.

While Blake went to round up the dogs, the rest of us passed through the sliding glass doors to the deck. Smoke billowed and churned while glowing, hissing embers landed in the pool.

We made quite a crowd, with me, Santi, Reynold, Anjali, Penelope, Vladimir, Summery—and of course Carl, Farrell, Yma, and Totoro. Not to mention Blake, Alpha, Beta, and Russell. I hoped Anjali was right and Reynold had ordered the *biggest* and *best* helicopter, because we were going to need a lot of room.

Reynold still clutched his phone and tablet, even though they were useless without Wi-Fi. Despite the fact that I'd been basically living without a phone for weeks, it was weird seeing that many people just sit there without tapping and staring at screens. Vladimir leaned on the railing, watching the sky as if it was possible to see something, while Reynold and Anjali sat next to each other on an ash-covered couch. Penelope, Summery, and I petted the animals to keep them calm— not that the fat cat making my chest all sweaty seemed to have any problem relaxing. Totoro liked being swaddled so much, I think he must have been a human baby in a previous life.

Then Penelope turned pale as a new moon. "Look," she whispered.

The gray smoke brightened as an orange wall of fire broke through only a couple hundred yards from the house. Before, the approaching fire had just been a bright glow, but now I could see individual flames hungrily licking the sides of trees and devouring the dry grass and bushes. It really did sound like a train, so loud all it needed was an air horn to be complete.

High above, we heard the *WHAP WHAP WHAP* of helicopter blades.

"Finally!" squeaked Santi.

Where was Blake? He still hadn't come out with the dogs. I ran back inside, yelling his name as loud as I could.

"I'm in here," he answered, and I followed his voice to the garage.

He had Alpha and Beta on leashes, but Russell's homemade version had gotten lost somewhere, probably while the three of them were playing.

"I'm trying to find another collar and leash for Russell so he doesn't run away from the helicopter," said Blake, frantically digging through a drawer in the workbench.

If you asked me, the workbench had never been used for actual work. The tools still had price tags, and some of them were in the original plastic.

"There's no time," I said. "The helicopter's here. Penelope will have to keep him calm."

Then I called Russell, "Come on, boy! Come on! Who's a good boy?"

The scarred brown-and-white dog trotted toward me, wagging his stump of a tail, and we all ran back outside.

The helicopter was lower and louder, the churning force of its blades whipping our hair and clothes and actually clearing some of the smoke. But we still couldn't see it—and it couldn't see us.

"We're here!" I yelled.

As everyone else joined in, jumping up and down and waving their arms, we looked like the saddest exercise class you've ever seen.

"HERE WE ARE! RIGHT HERE! WE'RE UNDERNEATH YOU!"

But there was no sign if the pilot heard us. She seemed to be hovering in place, looking for somewhere to land or lower a line. Without being able to talk to her, there was no way we could tell her how close she was.

The smoke shifted, and for a moment I saw the orange-and-white body of the helicopter—farther above and to the side than I'd thought—and then the smoke came back, and it disappeared.

The *WHAP WHAP WHAP* became a *WHAP WHAP WHAP* and then a *WHAP WHAP WHAP*.

"It's flying away!" I said, my heart sinking as fast as the helicopter was rising.

"Get back here!" raged Reynold. "I'm not paying you to fly away! I'M PAYING YOU TO RESCUE US!"

But it was no use.

"If pilot cannot see us, pilot cannot rescue us," said Vladimir quietly. "Too much risk for crew."

Without the helicopter noise, the fire roared louder than ever. It looked closer than ever, too.

I think Santi summed up the way we all felt when he started crying, his high, thin wail barely audible over the rampaging wildfire.

CHAPTER TWENTY-FOUR
Not Rescued

What do we do now, Dad?" asked Blake, looking truly scared for the first time.

In the living room, Reynold stared at the useless tablet in his hands, his expression completely blank, and suddenly I saw how he would have needed his brother and sister. He may have had the bossy personality of a leader, but he didn't seem to have enough ideas of his own. I think he literally had no clue what to do next.

"Don't quit on us now, Reynold," said Anjali, gripping his arm.

"Maybe Vladimir can try to get the generator going again," he said in a voice so quiet it was almost a whisper. "If we can get the Wi-Fi working, we can tell the helicopter our coordinates . . . Maybe they'll come back."

The big manny shook his head. "Generator is impossible."

Penelope rolled her eyes. "This is so typical of you, Reynold. You're great at building something amazing, something people desperately want, but you never think about how it will work in the real world. You constructed this perfect glass fortress in the forest, and now what? When the power goes out, you might as well be living in a cooking pot, waiting to boil. Well, guess what? Nobody's coming to rescue us. Sometimes you have to do things yourself!"

Just then, there was a loud *THUMP*.

"Was that a tree? Did a tree just fall on the house?" asked Summery in a shaky voice.

As Alpha and Beta started barking, there was another *THUMP*, and then another. And then still another. The sounds were coming from the front door.

"Those aren't trees," I said, pushing past Reynold and running toward the door with Blake and Santi right behind me.

As we reached the entryway, there was the loudest *THUMP* yet, followed by a ripping sound as the head of an axe tore through the stout wooden door. The axe head wiggled, squeaked, and disappeared, then sliced through again, sending long splinters flying.

By now, everyone was behind us, and all three dogs

were barking furiously. The axe was working its way around the locking mechanism—finally, the blade did enough damage that a big kick, delivered by a large booted foot, was enough to swing the door inward in a cloud of smoke.

In the doorway stood Lyndon Berthold. A wet bandana covered his nose and mouth, and ashes and soot covered everything else.

"Sorry, but the doorbell didn't work," he said.

"Do you know how much that door *cost*?" demanded Reynold.

Lyndon shook his head. "Don't know, don't care. I heard the helicopter and figured you were leaving without me. You would have, wouldn't you?"

"I figured you wouldn't want to go!" shouted Reynold. "I thought you were going to stay with your precious wooden house!"

"I'll build another—after all, I have plenty of ideas," said Lyndon.

"Don't you start with me," warned Reynold.

"Why shouldn't he start with you, when you're always starting with him?" said Penelope, moving closer.

She had always seemed like the calm one to me, but now she looked like she was about to lose her temper, too. Siblings have a way of making you do that, but in the middle of a forest fire, even I could postpone my issues with Santi until we got back to the compound.

If we got back to the compound.

Suddenly the little guy didn't seem so bad. I patted him on the head, and he looked up at me hopefully.

I turned to Blake, Vladimir, and Summery. "We need to leave in two minutes. Are you all ready to go?"

"Born ready," said Summery.

"I am hired to protect Blake, and that is one job," said Vladimir with a salute.

"I think you mean 'job one,'" I said. "But I know what you mean. Now let's go."

While the siblings argued in the living room and Anjali looked on helplessly, the rest of us gathered the supplies we needed for one last dash through the forest. Blake found backpacks, and we loaded them with bottled water, flashlights, and a first aid kit. Then we cut sheets into squares, soaked them in water, and tied the makeshift bandanas around our mouths and noses as Lyndon had done.

"Now get in shower," said Vladimir.

"Can't we shower after we get out of the forest fire?" groaned Blake.

But I saw what his bodyguard wanted.

"Quick, Blake. Do it with all your clothes on. Let's all get soaking wet. It's going to be hot out there."

We hurried to the nearest bathroom to wet ourselves down—but the shower controls were electronic. The water wouldn't even come on.

"Jump into the swimming pool!" said Santi.

We yelled at the other grown-ups to join us, but they were lost in their argument. I heard phrases like *you always* and *you never* and *for the last time*, and it made me think that, if they didn't get moving, it really would be the last time they argued. Were they going to stand there screaming at each other while the house burned down around them?

I tried not to think about Santi's pee as we all plunged into the pool, the dogs too, and then climbed out, getting a second soaking as the dogs shook water out of their fur. Totoro wasn't happy about getting wet, but I wanted to keep him safe, and he didn't mind too much as long as he stayed swaddled in the carrier.

We went back into the living room. If Reynold, Penelope, and Lyndon noticed the water streaming from our clothes, they didn't show it.

"All I ever wanted was to be recognized for the code I wrote!" said Lyndon.

"And I just wanted you to acknowledge the design concepts I came up with!" added Penelope.

"You wanted money!" screeched Reynold.

"We wanted to work together!" chorused his siblings.

"Time to go, dorks," I interrupted.

"We're not going anywhere until we settle this!" said Reynold.

"You might want to reconsider, Dad," said Blake as we all noticed an orange flicker on the walls.

Outside the window, the trees were burning like giant torches.

"Jump in the pool, and then let's get going!" I yelled.

And for once, Reynold, Penelope, and Lyndon didn't argue.

● ● ●

WE HAD TO get back to the compound to warn Trent and Leya the fire was coming. But with the forest quickly becoming a smoke-filled inferno, I wasn't sure I'd even be able to find the path. What if I accidentally led us right into the flames?

Fortunately, Blake and Lyndon had been over this terrain hundreds of times and could probably recognize landmarks even in the worst of situations, which was definitely the situation we were in.

"Come on, Uncle Lyndon!" said Blake, pulling him away from Reynold before the brothers started bickering again.

Blake and Lyndon led the group, with me and

Santi right behind, and Penelope, Reynold, Anjali, and Summery in the middle, and Vladimir making sure no one fell behind. Blake held the leashes for Alpha and Beta, Summery carried Carl, and Penelope walked with Russell while Yma clung to her shoulder and Farrell burrowed into her pocket. I still had Totoro in the sling and was surprised at how much a cat could weigh—my back was starting to hurt a little.

As we hurried along, fire leaped from treetop to treetop on either side of us, and flaming branches and pine cones dropped like missiles, igniting small fires wherever they landed. It made me sad to think about how this forest, which must have taken hundreds or even thousands of years to grow, was going to get wiped out in just one day.

Reynold was sad, too, but for a different reason.

"I'll never find another forest like this," he moaned to no one in particular. "Do you know how much it will cost to buy one? Old-growth redwood forests on private land don't exactly grow on trees, you know."

Even Anjali seemed to be getting tired of him. "Hopefully we'll live to go forest shopping another day," she snapped.

Lyndon and Blake stopped so fast I almost bumped into them.

"What's going on?" I asked.

"I think we're going the right direction, but I'm not a

hundred percent sure," said Lyndon, scanning from side to side. The smoke was now so thick it was hard to see fifty yards ahead.

"I think it's that way," said Blake, pointing right.

Lyndon nodded to the left. "Pretty sure it's that way."

Seeing a perfectly sized walking stick just a little distance from the group, I went over and picked it up, thinking it would help relieve the pressure on my aching back. It was just the right size, but no sooner had I put it down than it was yanked out of my hand so violently I almost fell over.

I stared, mouth agape, as the stick flew up into the sky, whipped by a taut rope snare that had been entirely undetectable under the layers of forest dandruff and ash. My ankles twitched as I recognized the same kind of trap that had caught me.

"That's mine!" said Lyndon excitedly. "Now I know exactly where we are."

"That could have been any one of us instead of a stupid stick," I yelled. "What is *wrong* with you?"

Lyndon shrugged. "This is my land, my part of the forest."

"Well, I hope you're happy about all the time you wasted fighting over it," I snarled as we started moving again, more quickly now that Lyndon had figured out where he was going.

Depending on the terrain, we moved at a fast walk or a slow run. Everyone understood the danger, and nobody needed to be told to go faster, although Reynold and Anjali were struggling a little, and I wondered if it was because they were used to traveling by jet and private car and not by good old-fashioned foot power.

Alpha and Beta were barking and pulling on their leashes, frenzied with excitement, but Russell was obediently sticking close to Penelope. All the animals seemed to know something was wrong. I almost wondered if they would have a better chance of surviving if we let them go—but I didn't want to risk it. What if we turned the dogs loose and they ran right back into the flames because they wanted to go home?

Lyndon was moving faster and faster, crashing through the brush, sometimes getting just far enough ahead that he became a blurry silhouette.

"Slow down, Lyndon," called Reynold, panting as he tried to keep up.

And then, just like that, Lyndon disappeared.

CHAPTER TWENTY-FIVE
The Final Traps

Lyndon had disappeared, and Blake was standing stock-still while his barking dogs jumped and pulled on their leashes. After a few more steps, I caught up and saw what Blake was staring at.

His uncle had fallen into a deep hole with smooth sides, one that had until a moment ago been covered by a blanket and dirt and leaves and been made to look like part of the forest floor. In other words, he'd been caught in a trap he'd made himself.

Lyndon was sitting on the floor of the pit, his legs out in front of him, massaging his kneecap.

"I hurt my knee," he groaned, looking up at us.

Soon everyone was crowded around.

"That's the same pit I fell into," muttered Blake.

"It serves you right!" cackled Reynold. "You've fallen prey to your own paranoid tendencies!"

"Now isn't the time," murmured Anjali.

"Even I have to admit he's right, Lyndon," said Penelope, shaking her head sadly and scratching Farrell's tiny chin.

"WILL YOU ALL STOP IT?" I yelled, exasperated. "We have to get him out NOW."

"Can you stand on knee?" asked Vladimir, crouching down.

Nodding, Lyndon climbed slowly to his feet, white-faced with pain. But it was still another six feet from the top of his outstretched fingers to the top of the pit—none of us had arms long enough to reach him.

"Actually, he's probably safe enough down there," said Reynold. "My bet is the fire will go right over him."

"You can't know that," said Summery, looking aghast while she clutched Carl.

"But if we stay here, we'll all fry with him."

"You know what?" said the Bertholds' cook. "You're a horrible person, Reynold. I quit. I'm no longer working for you, effective immediately."

"You can't quit; you're fired!"

"I did quit, and everybody heard me. You can't fire someone who's already quit, you big jerk."

Blake stepped up to his dad and shoved him. "Dad,

we can't leave Uncle Lyndon down there. That would be like murder or something."

"He dug the pit, not me," said Reynold, folding his arms.

Penelope looked down anxiously at her brother. "Are you sure you can't climb out?"

Lyndon just shook his head.

The fire was now so close it felt like we were standing in front of a thousand open pizza ovens. The air shimmered and rippled in the heat. My clothes, which had been sopping wet when we left Blake's house, were now barely damp, and the bandana covering the lower part of my face had almost completely dried out.

We had maybe a couple minutes before the fire swept over all of us.

"The dog leeches," said Vladimir, quickly unhooking Alpha and Beta's leashes and knotting them. Together they were maybe twelve feet—long enough to reach Lyndon, but not long enough for him to wrap it around himself or for all of us to pull on.

Then I had an idea. "Summery, if you're carrying Carl, he doesn't need his leash, does he?"

"I guess not," she said.

I was already untying the piece of rope we'd fastened around his neck. Added to the leashes, we had just enough.

"Tie it around yourself," I called to Lyndon as I tossed one end down.

He figured that out fast, looping the line around his waist and then under his thighs so it would support his weight.

Vladimir stationed himself on the edge and set his feet, while behind him, the rest of us grabbed as much rope as we could.

"Counting three," said Vladimir. "One—"

"Forget that, pull now!" I yelled, and we all heaved as hard as we could.

Lyndon's weight on the other end felt like a box of bricks, but when we all took a small step backward, I knew it was working. Step by step, we struggled and strained and raised him from the hole.

I think he basically walked up the side of it while we pulled, because he came out standing up. Seeing him balanced on the edge, Reynold said, "Finally! Now let's get moving"—and let go of the rope.

I saw panic on Lyndon's face as he started to fall backward. I grabbed the rope as tightly as I could, but other people, hearing Reynold, had let go, too, and my sneakers started to slide toward the edge.

Calmly, Vladimir shot out a hand and grabbed Lyndon by the front of his checked shirt, gathered a big fistful of fabric, and pulled him to safety.

Then the chiseled man-mountain give his boss a disgusted look. "I quit also."

Reynold's self-righteous anger finally started to leave him.

"Really?" he squeaked.

Poor Blake looked so embarrassed I wondered if he was next. But kids can't really quit their families. Only adults like Kristen get to do that.

. . .

AFTER THAT WE just ran as fast as we could, totally disorganized, with the fire behind and above and beside us—I didn't want to think about what would happen if it closed in ahead of us. I could tell Lyndon's knee was hurting, but he kept hobbling and didn't complain once. We didn't have time to untie the dogs' leashes, so fortunately they stayed close to the pack. In fact, sometimes they were a little too close. I almost tripped over Russell more than once when he practically ran under my feet.

Then I heard a familiar bowling-alley rumble and looked off to my left.

"You have GOT to be kidding me," I said, before yelling, "EVERYBODY, LOOK OUT!"

One of us had blundered into the mother of all log traps, and now a dozen massive trunks were crashing down the hill toward us, blazing with bright orange flames.

"Behind the biggest tree!" shouted Lyndon, which was confusing at first because there were huge trees everywhere, and some of them were on fire.

But there was a monster trunk a short sprint ahead. Waving at everyone to follow, I made it there and flattened myself against it on the side opposite the tumbling, flaming logs.

We huddled there as the logs crashed into it, making the tree tremble and throwing off sparks on either side. I was afraid the force would be strong enough to topple even this towering redwood, but the tree held firm. Once the immediate danger had passed, we started jogging again.

"You know what?" said Penelope. "I quit, too. Lyndon and Reynold, you guys are going to have to work out your issues without me. You're both one hundred percent bananas."

"He's bananas, not me," rasped Reynold, stumbling forward.

"Maybe a little bit bananas," Anjali muttered.

"You're ALL bananas," I said. "But can we please just escape now and settle it later?"

"I'm not the one who digs holes and falls into them," grumbled Reynold.

"At least I don't take credit for other people's ideas," growled Lyndon. "You got all that stuff about the inter-connectedness of the natural world from me."

"STOP ARGUING!" yelled Santi, which surprised everyone so much it actually worked.

We kept going. Unless we had gotten turned around in the smoke, we had to be close to the fence. But where was it?

I heard something over the roar of the fire. It was kind of an animal sound, like whales, but not whales—after all, Penelope's stereo had to have been incinerated by now. From the way their ears perked up, the dogs heard it, too.

It was low and weird, almost like moaning wind. What was it?

Then, just barely, I heard human voices, too.

"Dagmar . . . Santi . . ."

"Trent and Leya are calling for us!" I told Santi. "We're almost there!"

"MOM! DAD!" bellowed Santi, his stocky little legs suddenly moving faster than they ever had before.

"Santi!" called Leya, followed by a string of the Span-ish she only uses when she's really happy or upset.

"Run, Dagmar, run!" I heard Trent yell.

The smoke cleared, and we saw them silhouetted against the fence. It felt like some weird dream as we ran the final yards, then tried and failed to hug them through the fence—basically, our hands hugged, because the rest of us wouldn't fit through.

Their eyes widened when they saw all the people and animals with us, so I just said, "Blake's family. I'll tell you the rest later."

"The gate's over here!" called Blake, running to it and keying in the code.

When it didn't unlock, he tried again. And again.

But the gate wouldn't open.

CHAPTER TWENTY-SIX
The Last Roundup

The power's still out!" I said, once again amazed at how nothing the Bertholds owned worked without electricity. "We'll have to go over or under."

Vladimir was shaking and kicking the gate, trying to break it open, but it wouldn't budge.

Reynold eyed the top of the fence and shook his head. "Don't expect me to climb that thing."

"There's no time to dig under it," said Penelope in a panic. "And we can't get the dogs over. Dogs can't climb fences!"

Santi was trying to crawl under it like he'd done before. But the fence was tighter here, and he couldn't even get an arm through. On the other side, Leya started digging with her hands.

The fire's crackling sound made me think of a demon

ripping and devouring the wood. Was this as far as we would make it? Were we doomed to get grilled against the fence?

Trent was the only one not panicking. After all, he'd broken into hundreds of abandoned places. While we were all acting like headless chickens, he studied the gate. Then, with a quick shake of his head, he pulled his multi-tool out of the sheath on his belt, unfolded it, and calmly started snipping wires on the part of the fence *next* to the gate.

When he saw what Trent was doing, Reynold started shoving his way through. Trent tried to stop him with a simple "Wait!" but when that didn't work, Vladimir grabbed the billionaire and held him back until Trent was finished.

"Kids first," said Trent, peeling back a section of fence big enough for Santi to walk through upright.

Santi went through, followed by me and then Blake.

"Then the women, just to be polite," said Trent, and Summery, Penelope, and Anjali doubled over and scrambled through, trying not to snag themselves on the cut ends of the fence.

I'm pretty sure Trent would have said, *And now the dogs,* except Alpha, Beta, and Russell had already snaked through, leaving only Reynold, Lyndon, and Vladimir.

When Vladimir released his hold, Reynold charged

for the hole in the fence at the exact same moment as Lyndon, and they both got stuck in the opening with Vladimir behind them.

"Ow! Ow! Ow!" yelped Reynold as the poky parts of the fence jabbed him.

"You moron!" snarled Lyndon.

The more they struggled, the more it hurt, and the longer Vladimir was trapped on the other side.

Over the noise they were making, I heard it again— that weird moaning sound. It was a lot louder now.

Looking completely exasperated, Vladimir put a big foot on Reynold's butt and pushed hard, sending both of the men through the fence to the other side, scratched and howling.

"YOWWWWWW!" they cried.

Dropping to all fours, the big Exurbistanian worked his way through the gap while Trent and I pulled back on the fence to try to make more room. I think Vladimir was as big as Trent and Leya and Santi and me all put together.

We stumbled into the pasture, feeling relieved to be out of the forest. The air was still hazy but a little bit clearer there.

Leya hugged and kissed Santi, then hugged and kissed me, too. "I was worried to death!" she said, over and over.

Trent ran his fingers through my hair, then frowned and pulled out a piece of smoking bark. "You gave us a real scare, but I knew you'd come through," he said before announcing, "Introductions later. Everyone, follow me!"

As we headed for the muddy creek, I heard the sound again. We all did. And just as I realized what it was, the herd of brown-and-white cows came mooing and lowing toward us, a lot more nervous than they'd been that morning.

"Look out!" yelped Reynold.

"For what?" asked Trent, looking around.

"Those . . . things!" said Reynold, pointing.

"They're just cows," said Leya. "Herefords, to be precise."

"Come on, everybody, let's go," urged Blake.

Then there was a whistle so loud we all stopped and covered our ears.

"Wait a minute!" said Penelope, taking her fingers out of her mouth.

"What is it now?" asked Blake.

"These beautiful cows," said Penelope. "We can't just leave them here."

■ ■ ■

"You have got to be kidding," said Blake, staring at the herd of almost two dozen cattle, which were looking back at us with round, worried eyes.

I'd always assumed cows were dumb animals—heck, the word *bovine* is used to describe *the characteristic of placidity or dullness*. But if I could have read the thoughts of these ruminants, I'm guessing they would have been thinking something like, *If these humans don't take us along, we'll trample them.* Which got me wondering whether it would be better to be burned up in a forest fire or run over by a herd of cattle, and I really didn't have time to think about that.

I had no idea how we could possibly rescue a bunch of cows, but it did seem awful to leave them there to become roast beef. I mean, if they became roast beef eventually, I would probably be willing to have a sandwich, but there was no chance of that happening here.

"The woman with the bird and the squirrel is right," said Leya. "We have to take them with us."

When Trent looked at Leya, the expression on his face was similar to the one he wore when she unveiled a new art project, which made me wonder if he really liked her art. But he obviously loved her, because he always *said* he liked it. Which got me thinking more about how maybe you didn't always have to like the people you loved, or even think their ideas were any good—if they were family, you just had to back them up.

"I don't suppose there are any wranglers among us?" asked Summery, who seemed to be counting the cows in her head.

"My grandfather and grandmother had a ranch, and I used to spend summers there as a little girl," said Leya.

"Well, I'd say you're in charge of this roundup," said Trent.

Leya frowned. "But they also had horses."

"We don't have time for this!" insisted Reynold.

Lyndon looked at his brother, shook his head, and cleared his throat. "I can't believe I'm saying this, but I agree with Reynold."

On the far side of the pasture, the forest was blazing right up to the fence. A huge gust of wind shook the treetops and fanned the flames to heights we hadn't seen before. Flaming pine cones, needles, and branches sailed into the pasture.

The cows mooed uneasily. It looked to me like they might stampede at any moment.

"Spread out, all of you!" ordered Leya. "Make a half circle behind the cows. We'll walk forward together."

As people reluctantly obeyed, Santi pulled so hard

on Leya's hand I thought she might fall over. "What if they bite us? What if they attack?"

"Cows do not attack," she said simply.

I sneaked up behind him and whispered in his ear. "Usually."

Leya's plan worked. We fanned out, and with loud whistles from Penelope and Blake, who were best at that, we all started moving forward with the cows leading the way, followed by us and our odd menagerie. Alpha and Beta suddenly got the idea and ran along either side of the herd, barking at any cows who started to stray. Russell wanted in, too, but he wasn't quite as good at it, and Penelope had to call him back.

Gaining speed as we went, we crossed the rest of the pasture, splatted through the muddy creek, and reached the compound. The clumsy cows trampled our lawn chairs, my sleeping area, and even Leya's art installation before we could stop them, but no one got mad because we obviously had bigger problems to deal with.

"Herd them toward the wall!" shouted Leya.

I never would have guessed it, but Trent's wall had a purpose after all, serving as half of a corral where we could pen the cows until we figured out what to do next. Alpha and Beta prowled in front of the open side, making sure the cows didn't escape.

"Do cell phones work here?" asked Reynold.

I shook my head.

"I told you that we should have built our own cell tower," scolded Anjali.

"So now what do we do?" asked Blake. "The fire is just going to keep coming."

"Everybody stay calm while we have a quick meeting," said Trent.

"Calm? Calm?!? That's easy for you to say, buddy—your hundred-million-dollar mansion isn't burning in the woods," sputtered Reynold.

"As if your home is more important than anyone else's!" said Lyndon. "I built MY house with MY OWN HANDS. Forget I ever agreed with you!"

"The two of you aren't invited to this meeting," I said. "Everyone else can come."

While Reynold and Lyndon quarreled, the rest of us stepped off to the side and formed a circle.

"Well, Dagmar," said Trent grimly, "you've been wanting to leave all summer. I guess you finally got your wish."

"If this is how wishes come true, I would have wished for something else," I told him.

"Vladimir, what do you think we should do?" asked Anjali. "After all, you have military training."

Vladimir squinted. "Fortify position and radio reinforcements."

"We can't stay here," said Summery. "And we don't even have a radio."

"This is not military situation," agreed Vladimir.

"We need to rescue ourselves," I said as Trent, Leya, and others nodded their heads.

"And how do you think we should do that?" asked Leya.

"I have a plan," I said.

CHAPTER TWENTY-SEVEN
Tree!

All right, let's get to work," said Trent, clapping his hands.

I had expected the grown-ups to say *No* or *But* or *Wait a minute, that will never work,* but instead they listened and accepted my plan without suggesting a single change. As we prepared to put it into action, I almost wished they had, because if it didn't work, it would be all my fault.

On the other hand, if it did, I would be saving the lives of eleven humans, seven pets, and approximately two dozen cows.

The first thing we did was put all the animals except for Alpha and Beta—and the cows, obviously—inside Helen Wheels. When I finally unknotted the scarf that held Totoro to my chest during our escape through the woods, both the cat and I were completely soaked in my sweat. Cats are great for warming up on a cool evening, but carrying one through a forest fire is like doing a fun run in the desert with a hot water bottle in your shirt.

I gave him a couple quick pets and scooted him inside while Penelope did the same with Farrell, Carl, Yma, and Russell.

"Won't the cat try to catch the bird?" I asked as we closed the door behind them.

Penelope just laughed. "Totoro? He has a hard time catching cat food."

Next, we grabbed everything we could find that held water—from the plastic bucket and watering can to food tubs and our big cooler—and formed a bucket brigade stretching from the pump to the compound. We put Lyndon and Reynold on opposite ends so they wouldn't argue, and while Lyndon worked the pump and filled the containers, Penelope grabbed each one and handed it along to Summery, who handed it to Leya, who handed it to Santi, who handed it to Anjali, who handed it to Reynold, who handed it to Blake, who handed it to me.

Each person had to do a little running between hand-offs, but the system still worked a lot more smoothly than if we'd all been doing our own filling and carrying.

When the containers reached me, I carried them up a ladder and splashed them over the wooden shingles and sides of the house, soaking it as well as I could—realizing when I saw a soggy coatimundi that one of the windows was still open and water was getting inside.

After the house was completely drenched, I stowed the filled bucket, tubs, and cooler in the back of the truck, in case we needed more water later. Then I collapsed the extendable aluminum ladder and put that in, too.

Meanwhile, Trent and Vladimir had been busy getting the house ready to roll. It was still on the trailer, so it already had wheels, but after arriving at our new location, Trent had wedged jacks and cinder blocks underneath so we could walk around inside without it rocking back and forth. Now all that stuff had to be pulled out and tossed aside so we could tow it back to the road.

When the bucket brigade's work was done, I raced back along the line.

"We're almost ready!" I told everyone. "Give yourself a good soaking before we go!"

We took turns working the pump so we could all get completely wet again. After the heat and wind and ash and smoke, it felt so good to stick my head under the cool, rushing water.

If we make it out of this fire, the first thing I want to do is go to the beach, I thought. I didn't even care if it was a cold beach. I just wanted to be wet and chilly and to breathe clean air.

As we gathered back by Helen Wheels, the only support still in place was a jack that held up the trailer tongue. All Trent had to do was back his pickup into place so we could hitch them together.

The cows were mooing again, moving around restlessly, and it was all the dogs could do to keep them in place. Smoke had blanketed the pasture and was getting so thick I could hardly see out of the compound.

Then, above us, I heard the droning of a plane's engines. It got closer and closer and, when it seemed to be above the Bertholds' forest, turned and started pulling away.

"I'll bet that's a Cal Fire plane," said Trent. "They probably just dropped a big load of retardant."

"Hooray! Finally!" I cheered as Blake, Santi, and a few others joined in.

"I ordered a helicopter, not a plane," fumed Reynold.

"The firefighters don't work for you," Summery reminded him. "Just like me and Vladimir."

"We can't wait for them, because they might not even know we're here," I said.

"Trent, back up the truck," urged Leya.

Trent hurried over, climbed in, and—

Nothing happened.

Through the window, I could see Trent pound the steering wheel with his fist.

"Uh-oh," said Santi.

Trent turned the key again. The starter turned over, but the engine didn't seem to want to catch.

I was beginning to wonder if we could possibly hitch the cows to Helen Wheels and have them pull us to safety when the engine finally roared to life.

Now we really cheered. Everyone watched as Trent, guided by Leya and Vladimir, slowly backed the truck into place. It took way too long, because first he was at the wrong angle, then he was too far off to the side, but eventually he had it lined up so the knob on the trailer hitch was directly underneath the tongue of the trailer. Leaving the engine running, he hopped out while Leya lowered the jack until the trailer and truck were connected.

The fire had crossed the pasture by now and was closing in on the compound. Ribbons of smoke streamed toward us while the hot wind raised the temperature from open-oven to blast-furnace. It was time to go.

"All right, everybody in!" I shouted, throwing open the door to Helen Wheels.

Nobody moved. Reynold, Anjali, Lyndon, and Penelope all just looked at each other.

"You want us to go inside that . . . tiny . . . *house*?" asked Reynold, blinking.

"That's right," I told him.

"I presumed I would at least get to ride in the truck," he said.

"Daaaad," groaned Blake, kicking the dirt in embarrassment.

I took a deep breath and was ready to yell something really rude, but fortunately Leya saved the day.

"We would be honored to have you in our home, however small it may be," she said. "Please, won't you be our guests?"

Even someone as rude as Reynold Berthold couldn't refuse that kind of hospitality, so while I held the door open, Reynold, Anjali, Lyndon, Penelope, and Summery all climbed inside.

Leya started to follow, but Trent grabbed her arm. "Don't you want to ride up front?"

"Despite the circumstances, we are their hosts," she said. "Santi and I will ride with them."

It was definitely going to be a tight squeeze. Helen Wheels was cozy enough with just four humans and no pets—now it was going to be like having a book club meeting in a phone booth.

Suddenly, there was the biggest gust of wind yet, and the air around us filled with smoke, ash, and glowing pine needles. Smoldering pine cones thudded against the roof and walls of Helen Wheels as the cows surged and lowed in their makeshift pen.

"Time to go—now!" shouted Trent as one of the cows escaped past the frantic dogs and galloped down the road.

Santi and Leya jumped into the house while Trent ran for the truck and Vladimir quickly attached the chains to the trailer.

Blake and I had one more job to do before we could climb in the truck: herd cows.

First, we called Alpha and Beta back. Then, yelling and waving our arms, we tried to drive the cows out of the pen and down the road after their escaped friend. But they didn't go anywhere. From their frightened bellows and rolling eyes, it was obvious they were confused and terrified. And the thunder of the approaching fire was so loud it practically drowned out our voices.

All of a sudden, I wished Leya wasn't inside the house. And that we had horses. And real cowboys. And, while I was dreaming of things we didn't have, private helicopters for each and every one of us, even the cows.

But we didn't have those things.

And the fire was getting closer.

Trent honked the horn and flashed his headlights. We had to move. But the cows weren't getting the message. Vladimir was right behind me and Blake, but his commando training clearly hadn't included a unit on how to motivate panicky farm animals.

Scared and exhausted, with no idea what to do next, I did something I'm not particularly proud of. I punched a cow.

Not in the face or anything—I hit it on its hindquarters, and I definitely hurt my hand more than I hurt the cow. But it worked! Suddenly, the cow started trotting up to the road. Seeing that, another cow followed. And another, and another, until the little herd was all headed the right direction.

"Yee-HAW!" I yelled.

"That was awesome!" shouted Blake, setting the dogs loose again.

"You are good cow puncher," said Vladimir admiringly.

Alpha and Beta streaked after the loping livestock as if they were born to do it, one dog on either side of the herd, although I'm not sure the cows had any intention of leaving the road.

Trent leaned on the horn again, reminding us not to stand there admiring the cows, and Blake and I ran back to the truck and piled in, squeezing onto the small bench seat in back. Vladimir took shotgun and slammed the door.

Revving the engine, Trent put the truck in gear and rolled slowly forward. Helen Wheels weighed four or five tons, even when it wasn't fully loaded.

"Um . . . guys?" said Vladimir, putting his face close to the windshield.

"What is it, Vlad?" asked Trent.

"Tree . . ."

"Three what?"

"No, tree!"

We looked. A line of fire was blazing up behind the cattle pen and heading right for the road. The wind was tossing all the trees hard, and one of them, its branches blazing, was starting to fall over.

When it crashed down in front of us, it would completely block the road.

CHAPTER TWENTY-EIGHT
The Tiny Fire

Trent stomped the accelerator so hard I was surprised his foot didn't go through the floorboard. The engine of his old truck roared, and the tachometer needle jumped into the red. But we didn't exactly peel out like a race car. Instead, the truck-and-trailer combo went from a walk to a jog to a slow run—heading straight for the part of the road that was about to be engulfed by a fallen, flaming tree.

"AaaaaaAAAAAAAHHHHHHHH!" screamed Blake, ducking down in the back seat and covering his eyes.

"NOOOOOOOOOOOOO!" I yelled, my eyes wide open and my fingers digging into the upholstery so hard I ripped the fabric and got foam under my fingernails.

"Maybe stop?" suggested Vladimir in a quiet, reasonable tone.

The cows and dogs had already cleared the spot where we were speeding to our certain doom. Trent gripped the steering wheel and kept the pedal to the floor while his eyes watched the toppling tree above us. It had started its descent slowly, as if its roots were reluctant to give up their grip on the soil, but now it was falling faster, just as we were accelerating toward where it was going to land.

What if it hit us?

What if it hit Helen Wheels?

What if it landed in the middle, trapping us on opposite sides?

"MAYBE STOP?" suggested Vladimir again, this time at the top of his lungs, as Trent's truck finally got going faster than any of us could run.

I could feel the trailer tugging on the truck and looked back to see Helen Wheels bouncing up and down and side to side on the dirt road. Santi was probably about to start barfing, if he hadn't already. Just thinking about somebody barfing in the tiny house made me want to barf, too, so I wished I hadn't thought of that. But maybe thoughts are contagious, because Blake opened his window, stuck his head out, and spewed all over the side of the truck.

I looked up. The tree was definitely going to hit us.

The engine roared.

"We're going to make it," Trent said calmly.

The tree swept down out of the sky, its burning branches like the brushes of a demonic car wash.

All four of us yelled together. I heard yelling from Helen Wheels, too. They definitely shouldn't have been looking out the windows.

I braced for impact. There was a deafening, heart-stopping CRUNCH . . . but we kept rolling. We had made it! I whipped around and looked out the back window of the cab. Helen Wheels had made it, too. It was still jouncing and bouncing along as we roared down the road with the fallen tree behind us flaming orange and red like an evil sunset.

Our screams of terror turned to shouts of relief. Trent honked the horn, and Vladimir and I pounded the ceiling as Blake pulled his head back in, wiped his mouth with the back of his hand, and smiled weakly.

"Maybe we're going to survive after all," he said.

"Forget maybe!" I told him. "We're definitely going to make it now!"

And then we all lurched forward when Trent stomped on the brakes.

• • •

EVEN THOUGH THE cows were being encouraged down the road by two giant dogs that barked and nipped at their hooves, they couldn't go as fast as a truck. As we accelerated away from death-in-the-form-of-a-flaming-falling-tree, we suddenly found the cows right in front of us, and if Trent hadn't reacted as quickly as he did, we would have turned the beeves into roadkill. (*Beeves: plural of beef.*)

This wasn't going to be a quick escape, after all. Instead of flying down the road at top speed—that is, the top speed of an old truck pulling a tiny house full of mammals—we were now forced to roll along at a pace so slow I could have jumped out and run faster. And thanks to the wind and the fallen tree, the fire had jumped the road and was now burning along both sides, spreading faster than we could drive.

Again I heard a plane overhead, but the smoke was just too thick to find it. Could they see us? Did they know we were there? Any fire crews in the area would definitely know about Blake Berthold's giant glass-and-steel mansion, but there was no way they knew about our tiny house, which wasn't even supposed to be there.

The narrow two-lane road went slightly downhill, giving me hope that we would drive out of the fire soon. After all, heat rises and fire goes up, right?

"Turn on radio," said Vladimir suddenly.

"This seems like an odd time to listen to music," said Trent.

"Not music—news update," said Vladimir, reaching for the dashboard to do it himself.

The first station he found was playing a dance track, and the volume was LOUD. It was weird to hear something so silly and normal while the forest was burning down around us. The next station was playing a sad country song, which seemed more appropriate, but still, not very useful.

After finding commercials, a baseball game, and a traffic report from a hundred miles away, Vladimir finally tuned in to a crackly local news station with a reporter giving updates about the fire.

"... *Cal Fire crews are mobilizing to attack the fast-moving blaze, which fortunately has started in a largely unpopulated area...*"

"Largely, but not ENTIRELY," I objected.

"Shh!" said Trent.

"... *although in dry, windy conditions, there is concern it could soon threaten nearby towns. Planes have already made several drops of slurry, and all residents of the affected areas are encouraged to seek safety immediately.*"

"No DUH," said Blake, and this time I shushed him before Trent could do it.

"*Do not stop, do not pass Go, just get out of there as fast as you can,*" said another voice on the broadcast, a man identified as a local fire official.

"Does he have any advice for people with cows?" I asked as the station cut to a commercial for, of all things, backyard barbecue grills.

It was agonizing to sit in the back seat and watch the waddling rumps of the cows as they trotted slowly down the road. But there was literally nothing I could do. Feeling antsy, I turned around and looked back at Helen Wheels.

The first thing I saw was Santi's round face pressed up against the kitchen window as he waved at me. He wasn't barfing. In fact, he looked happy, like he was on a school bus headed to a tour of a candy factory.

The second thing I saw was flames on the roof of the house.

"Helen Wheels is on fire!" I gasped.

"How bad is it?" asked Trent, checking his mirrors.

"So far, it's just on the roof," I told him.

All the work we had done to soak the house hadn't protected it for long. The fire was just so hot it dried everything out in minutes.

"I'll stop," said Trent, lifting his foot off the gas.

"Don't stop," said Vladimir, reaching over and pushing down on Trent's right knee, bringing the truck dangerously close to the cows.

"But we have to put that fire out!" said Trent, struggling to resist the pressure applied by the hand of the massive Exurbistanian.

"Fire is closing in," said Vladimir. "If you stop now, I think all our geese is cooked."

"But what about everyone inside Helen Wheels?" asked Trent desperately.

"What is Hell on Wheels?" asked Vladimir.

"That's the house's name," I told him.

Vladimir, puzzled, let go of Trent's leg. "Why do you name house?"

"Because . . . I'll tell you later. It's not important!" shouted Trent. "What is important is that we put that fire out."

"I agree with Vladimir," said Blake. "And not because he used to work for my dad or anything. If we stop on this road, we're going to bake like flatbread."

"That's a terrible analogy," I told him.

He shrugged. "I can't help it. Ever since that whole business about the wood-fired oven, when I thought we were getting flatbread for lunch, I haven't been able to stop thinking about it. I just hope I haven't eaten my last one ever."

While everyone was talking, the fire had been growing on the roof of Helen Wheels. Santi was still smiling and waving, the little dope, so he obviously had no idea. But even if we couldn't stop, we had to do something.

I slid open the little window at the back of the truck's cab. It was about the size of a microwave oven door, so I had no idea if I could make it, but putting my arms together like a diver, I wriggled my arms, head, and shoulders through before Trent realized what I was doing.

"Dagmar, don't!" he said, his voice barely audible because my body was blocking the opening.

I kept wiggling until my hands touched the bed of the truck and my hips were almost out of the window. The bottom edge was digging into my stomach, and I wasn't sure I could go any farther. But when my heels touched the roof of the cab, I pushed against it and tried to slide the rest of the way out.

It wasn't working. And the metal truck bed was so hot it hurt my hands. Even worse, I was in such an awkward position that I didn't think I could reverse direction and make it back into the truck.

Then I felt Blake's hands under my shins, lifting and pushing until I popped out of the window and slid onto my stomach in the back of the pickup.

Crouching, I looked around. The containers we'd filled were sloshing with water, although the bucket had fallen over and spilled when Trent hit the brakes.

I grabbed the empty bucket and dipped it into the cooler, filling it halfway. Balancing carefully, I inched back to the tailgate and threw the water up toward the flames. The water fanned out into ten thousand drops, and I could hear the fire sizzle. But I'd only scored a partial hit. Worse, most of the fire was high up and out of sight. I could throw all the water I wanted, and I wouldn't know if I was putting the fire out.

In front of me, the tiny window on the side of the tiny house slid open, and Santi's face was replaced by Leya's.

"Dagmar, what are you doing?" she asked.

"The roof's on fire. I'm putting it out," I told her.

"Tell your father to stop the truck, and we'll help you," she said.

I looked at the fire raging on either side of the road and shook my head. "We have to keep going. But I think I can do it."

"How on earth can you put the fire out from there?" she asked. Her voice sounded shaky, so I knew she was afraid, but I had no idea if she was more worried about me or about everyone inside.

"I'm not going to put it out from here," I said. "I'm coming over there. Now hold on."

CHAPTER TWENTY-NINE
Clean Air at Last

Standing in the back of a rolling pickup truck in the middle of a rapidly spreading forest fire behind a slowly clopping herd of cows is a place you would only expect to find yourself in a bad dream. But I was really there, and it was really happening. The fact that I also had to battle a tiny house fire only made the situation more surreal. The one thing that could have made it even worse was if it was like one of those dreams where you're in school and you're only wearing underwear. I was definitely wearing all my clothes—I just hoped they wouldn't catch fire.

I grabbed the ladder I had thrown into the back of the truck, extended it halfway, and put one end on the roof of Helen Wheels. The other end kept sliding around the truck bed, so I was relieved when Blake tumbled out of the cab window and said, "I'll hold it for you."

Now all I had to do was climb the ladder carrying enough buckets of water to put out the fire. Easy, right?

I filled the bucket two-thirds full this time, meaning it was even heavier than before. Then I carefully started climbing the ladder, feeling it shift with every bump and crack in the road. If the high end slipped off Helen Wheels' little peaked roof, I was going to hit the road as hard as a sack of beans dropped from a second-story window. It wouldn't kill me, but I definitely wouldn't be doing any more firefighting after that.

Rung by rung I went up until I reached the top of the house. The fire up there was about six feet in diameter and growing fast.

Leaning over the roof as far I could without falling, I slung the bucket, directing the water toward the lowest part of the fire. Direct hit! The part I'd soaked hissed and smoked before flaring up again. But at least it was weaker than before.

"Be careful!" scolded Leya as I scrambled back down.

Why do parents always say stuff like that? Who *wouldn't* be careful going down a ladder into the back of a moving vehicle?

"I'll think about it," I told her.

"How does it look?" asked Blake.

"Better," I said as I scooped more water from the cooler, which was now almost empty.

I went up the ladder again. The second bucket did more good than the first. I figured that, after three or four more direct hits, the little fire might stay out long enough for us to get away from the big fire.

This time I poured what was left in the cooler into the bucket, then topped it off with the contents of the plastic watering can. Unfortunately, just as I got to the top of the ladder again, the trailer hit a pothole, and the whole house swayed to one side, forcing me to drop the bucket and hold on to the roof for dear life with both hands.

For a long ten seconds, I thought the ladder was going to disappear from under me, leaving me dangling from the top of Helen Wheels, but at last it stabilized and I climbed back down to the truck.

"Are you okay?" asked Blake. "I thought you were going to fall!"

"I'm fine, but I wish I hadn't dropped the bucket," I told him.

"It's not like you have three hands," he said.

Coming from him, it sounded like a compliment.

Not having the bucket was a big problem. Now the only thing with a handle was the watering can, and a light sprinkle of water wasn't going to put out the fire. If I carried one of our remaining tubs in both hands, I wouldn't be able to hold on to the ladder.

That's when I realized the passenger door was open and Vladimir wasn't in his seat.

I heard his big feet slapping the asphalt and looked up to see him running alongside the truck, holding the bucket out to me.

"I accidentally kick bucket," he said, panting, "but then I pick it up."

I took it from him and watched in amazement as he grabbed the side of the truck and vaulted into the back, moving more gracefully than I would have expected from a man who looked about as fast as a refrigerator.

"Hurry!" he said, helping Blake hold the ladder steady.

Refilling the bucket from a big jar we usually used to make sun tea, I raced up the ladder, took careful aim, and hit the fire dead-on. There was nothing we could do about the forest burning around us, but this fire was going down.

After four more trips up and down the ladder, I was out of water—and the roof fire was out, too. Even better, we were finally ahead of the forest fire. We had come out of the woods into brown, grassy hills, and the wind was now blowing toward us, pushing the fire back while we moved forward.

Over the next mile, the air went from black to brown

to clear and breathable, and we could even see blue sky again. Behind us, the flames continued to swirl and rage, and a plume of smoke rose thousands of feet in the air, but we had escaped.

We could finally fill our lungs again. When we weren't coughing.

The first thing we saw was a Cal Fire truck with its lights flashing parked sideways across the road. It was obviously there to keep people from driving into the danger area. But the woman leaning against the truck and facing the other way wasn't expecting anyone to be coming *out* of the danger area. When she heard the first *MOO*, she jumped, and as she spun around, the look on her face as cows trotted past was one of pure astonishment.

She lifted her radio and started to speak into it, then dropped it and scrambled inside her truck when Trent laid on his horn.

"OUT OF THE WAY!" he bellowed.

As quickly as she could, the firefighter backed her truck out of the road, and we rolled past, the kids all waving and Russell barking out a window. Trent wasn't going to stop until we were totally safe.

The next thing we saw was a TV news truck with a reporter facing a camera and talking into a microphone. His back was to us, so he didn't see us coming, but the camera operator did—she pointed and said something, and he spun around and his mouth fell open like his jaw muscles had suddenly stopped working. Then the camera operator shoved him out of the way and aimed her camera at us, catching the cows, the dogs, the pickup truck, and the tiny house with the charred roof and faces filling the windows.

Recovering from his shock, the reporter started trotting alongside the truck, shouting questions as he held the microphone up to record our answers.

"Did you just come out of the fire?"

"I think that's pretty obvious," said Blake, back to his usual charming self.

"How does it look in there?"

"Everything is either flaming or smoking," I said.

"Are those your cows? Are you ranchers?"

"We picked them up along the way," I said. "We don't know who they belong to."

"She is good cow puncher," added Vladimir.

Trent still hadn't slowed down, and the reporter was having a hard time keeping up.

"Are any of you hurt?" he shouted, panting, just before Helen Wheels passed him.

It took me a minute to realize that, aside from Lyndon's twisted knee, nobody was. Eleven humans, seven pets, and a couple dozen livestock had escaped from a raging wildfire without serious injury. Yes, we were probably going to cough up crud for a week, and the heat from the fire had left my skin feeling toasted, like I'd spent a day at the beach without sunscreen, but I'd live. We'd *all* live. Literally.

"We're all okay!" I shouted to the reporter, adding, "Watch out for that—"

He didn't see it.

"—sign!"

I probably shouldn't have laughed just because a nicely dressed TV reporter with blow-dried hair ran straight into a road sign and dropped his microphone, but I couldn't help it. Neither could anybody else. After the day we'd had, it was a relief, and the truck and the house shook with laughter.

CHAPTER THIRTY
A Complete Write-Off

The fire had burned through the roof of Helen Wheels, leaving the sleeping loft a charred mess that stank of smoke. All of us, even the Bertholds, spent the first night in a middle-school gym that had been converted into an emergency shelter. Reynold complained the whole time about "the poor quality of the accommodations," from the sleeping cots to the bathrooms to the boxed meals provided by local volunteers, but there was nothing he could really do about it. He'd left without even his wallet, and had dropped his phone somewhere along the way, and it wasn't until the next day that he was able to reach his lawyer, who couriered some money that allowed them to escape to a four-star hotel. Until then, he had to live like the rest of us, and he didn't like it.

I thought maybe he would be changed by his near-death experience, or the fact that he and his siblings had all lost their houses at the same time, but if anything, he seemed more entitled and crabby than ever. I guess some people never change.

Blake, however, seemed to have fun at the shelter. He explored the school with me, played basketball on the playground, and even joined a cleanup crew organized by Trent and Leya. He was still kind of a jerk sometimes, but I had a feeling he wasn't going to turn out all bad.

The dogs, the cat, the coati, the parrot, and the squirrel weren't allowed into the gym, but people were nice about it and found places for them to stay overnight. The science lab had some old cages for Totoro, Carl, Yma, and Farrell, and the bike-storage area of the playground was turned into a temporary kennel where the dogs didn't seem too unhappy, judging from the sound of their barking.

A local rancher had taken the cows until their owner could be found. I never saw them again, although it's entirely possible I encountered them in the form of a delicious carne asada burrito.

When it came time for lights-out that first night, Reynold and Anjali chose cots in one corner of the gym while Penelope and Lyndon went to another. Vladimir and Summery picked a third corner, proving their resignations had been real. Even more interesting, the former bodyguard and cook put their cots right next to each other and held hands when they thought nobody was looking.

I decided to go say hi but called out to them on my way over so I wouldn't interrupt anything embarrassing.

"I just wanted to say thanks for all your help, Vladimir," I said. "And it was great meeting you, Summery, even if we were running for our lives."

Vladimir stood up, towering over me, and shook my hand. It felt like I was putting on a concrete boxing glove.

"You are welcome, Dagmar," he said. "You did very good job. I think you would be excellent bodyguard."

That was pretty great to hear. After all, Vladimir was one of the few grown-ups I knew who really had his act together.

"Where are you guys going after this?" I asked.

"Somewhere cool and wet," said Summery. "Maybe Alaska. Both of us can work anywhere. Restaurants are always hiring, and Vee is thinking about starting his own security firm."

I liked the way she called him Vee for short. It made me wonder whether they'd been going out for a long time, or if they'd always liked each other and just decided to go for it. Not that it was any of my business.

"Maybe you will work for me when you are older," said Vladimir.

"Maybe you'll work for *me*," I told him, just kidding around.

He smiled, which was new. "I would like that."

I gave them both hugs and said good night. When I woke up in the morning, they were gone.

■ ■ ■

BLAKE LEFT AFTER breakfast. A big, black SUV pulled up in front of the school while we were shooting baskets on the playground, and suddenly Reynold and Anjali were there, telling Blake it was time to go. I expected him to just turn around and walk away, but he didn't. He stared at the ball while he dribbled it with both hands.

I didn't know what to say, either, so I just said, "See you around, I guess."

"See you around," he said.

Where, exactly, I would see Blake Berthold, I had no idea.

He tossed me the ball before he jogged over to his parents.

"No, really!" he yelled over his shoulder. "I'll text you!"

I nodded, smiled, and shot the ball, making a perfect swish. Three points.

Then I felt my phone vibrate. Was Blake texting already?

It was Kristen. And she was *calling*.

"I saw it on the news, Dagmar—the news!" she said the moment I picked up. "Why didn't you call me?"

"It would have been the middle of the night for you," I said, feeling guilty that, with everything going on, I hadn't even thought about it.

"There's a viral video from the local news station that shows all of you going down the highway. And where did you get those cows?"

"They're not ours. We were just rescuing them."

"Well, my lawyer says this is proof your father is an unfit parent. You're coming to live with me in Zurich, Switzerland."

She was so mad and so loud I had to hold the phone away from my ear.

"Why Zurich?" I asked.

"I have to go there for work," she said, like it was the most obvious thing in the world. "And hold the phone closer. I can hardly hear you."

"But I don't want to go," I told her.

"We'll have a beautiful townhouse and a nice company car! You can't stay in the forest, anyway—according to the news, it burned down."

"I don't know anyone in Zurich."

"You'll know me."

I took a deep breath. Everything was happening so fast. If I wasn't careful, I was going to end up on the other side of the world.

"I miss you a lot," I told her. "But can I just wait a little bit to decide?"

"Of course you can," she said, not sounding very happy about it.

"I'll call you soon," I promised.

●●●

TRENT, LEYA, SANTI, and I stayed at the shelter for four days, until the fire had been put out or burned out and the ground had cooled where it started. Leaving Helen Wheels in the middle-school parking lot, we took Trent's truck back to the compound to see what was left. Really, nothing was. The fire had moved so quickly that most of the big trees were still standing, but it had burned so hot that it destroyed practically everything else in its path. All we found of Leya's art installation were a few blackened shreds of fabric. The lawn chairs were twisted, deformed aluminum tubes. My sleeping bag, the star lantern, the shade trellis— all gone.

Trent's wall, of course, was fine, even though it, too, was now sooty and black.

It gave me a funny feeling to see everything burned down to the ground. I had hated being there at the start of the summer, but now that it was all gone, I had a lonely, empty feeling inside, like we were truly homeless. Even Helen Wheels needed work before it would be habitable again.

HABITABLE: *capable of being lived in.*

"Let's go see Blake's house," I suggested.

"I don't see why not," said Trent.

It wasn't like we had anything to do or anyplace to be. We all piled back into the truck and drove around the charred, still-smoking forest until we found the Bertholds' winding driveway. At the end of it, the steel-and-glass spaceship house looked like it had crash-landed after a particularly rough trip through the galaxy. Glass was cracked, steel was twisted, and the chopped-open door hung askew.

"That poor family," said Leya, shaking her head.

"Are you thinking what I'm thinking, Dagmar?" asked Trent.

"Uh-huh," I said.

I know it sounds awful, but we were both thinking about unobtanium. It was unfortunate that the Bertholds' house was a ruin, of course. But something can always be salvaged from even the worst disaster.

We didn't go on an unobtanium hunt right then, however, because in front of the scorched smart mansion were parked three shiny new cars.

As we got out of Trent's old truck, I was surprised to see Blake, Reynold, Anjali, Lyndon, and Penelope all file out of the house.

"How does it look?" Trent called. As a fix-it guy, his first instinct was to ask whether something could be repaired.

"A complete write-off," answered Reynold. "The circuitry and wiring are all melted, and I suspect it's structurally unsound. I'm suing my architect for failing to anticipate the threat of fire and specify the necessary safety features."

"Sorry to hear it," said Trent, not sounding all that sorry, to be honest.

"Why are you guys here?" I asked Penelope and Lyndon.

"We told Reynold we wanted to talk this out one last time before we got the lawyers involved," said Penelope. "If he's willing to form a new corporation with the two of us as equal partners, then we won't have to pursue legal action."

"You guys really want to go into business with him?"

Penelope shrugged. "We haven't been very effective as a family. Maybe we'll do better as a business."

That sounded like a terrible idea. But it did give me a great one.

"Do you need a place to stay while you rebuild? Maybe Trent could make you tiny houses to stay in temporarily."

Penelope looked interested. "That's not a bad idea—although maybe instead of a *tiny* house, we could make it a *small* house?"

"And I could help him," said Lyndon, nodding. "There's plenty of lumber we can salvage. It might make a good project for all of us to team up on."

Reynold and Anjali looked at each other skeptically.

"I had been planning to buy another forest and commission another smart mansion from a different architect," he said. "But perhaps as an extremely short-term solution . . ."

Trent laughed, stepped forward, and held up his hands. "Thanks for the suggestion, Dagmar. I'll be very happy to refer the Bertholds to an excellent contractor, but we're not sticking around."

Santi looked up from where he had been digging in the ash with a stick, his clothes and face smudged with soot. "We're not?" he asked.

Trent looked at me and smiled. "Nope. We're going back to Oakland."

"But you need the work," I said.

"And you need Imani and Olivia and the rest of your friends," said Leya, giving my arm a squeeze. "I'm not sure we'd all be here if it weren't for your bravery and resourcefulness. Your father and I both agree you've earned the chance to go home."

I couldn't believe it. Trent and Leya had just told me we were going home, and everything around us was a wasteland of swirling ash. But now it actually sort of made sense to stay.

Everybody was watching me to see what I'd say next. And Blake actually laughed out loud when he heard it.

"Wait a minute," I said. "I have another plan."

CHAPTER THIRTY-ONE
This One Worked

It was a good plan, too. First, we got signed contracts from Reynold, Penelope, and Lyndon for Trent to build them small houses so they'd have places to stay while everyone figured out what came next. Then, after repairing the roof of Helen Wheels, we moved it onto their land near the remains of the spaceship. We all pitched in to salvage lumber, and the Bertholds paid Trent enough money that he was able to hire crews of workers from nearby towns to help the work go faster.

The fire had been bad, of course, but it wasn't quite as bad as it looked at first. After the wind blew away some of the ash, and a light rain fell one day, we could see a lot of green, growing things that had survived the conflagration. Most of the trees had lived, too, their bark charred but their trunks still strong and growing. It would take time, of course, but the forest would come back, and maybe its owners would appreciate it even more.

In early August, we moved back to Oakland. It felt amazing to see Imani, Olivia, Hailey, and Nevaeh again. Though it had only been a few months, I felt like we were all a whole year older. Even better, it was almost my birthday, and Imani told me she had my party all planned out—even though Olivia had tried to take over. Some things never change.

After a few days in a hotel, we found a new apartment and paid a whole year's rent in advance with the money Trent was earning. Helen Wheels stayed in the forest, and Trent commuted back and forth, spending weekends with us in Oakland and sleeping most weeknights at the job site.

Trent and Kristen seemed to have reached some kind of an agreement, helped by the fact that money suddenly wasn't an issue. She came back once, for a weekend in July, and took me to a spa in Napa Valley. It was good to see her, but the place was completely boring: how many mud packs and cucumber slices and pedicures and mixed-greens salads does one person need?

Since then, we'd texted every day, and Kristen promised the next time she came home, she'd stay for months. She said she'd be back again by Christmas, *maybe even*

Thanksgiving. But with Kristen it's best to just wait and see what happens.

Santi and I started school in mid-August with everyone else, and in some ways, it was like we'd never left—except I had a new friend I still hadn't quite told my old friends about. Before I went back to Oakland, Blake and I spent a lot of time coming up with new challenges for each other, but just for fun this time. He liked hanging around Trent and Lyndon, and even learned a little bit of carpentry.

Blake started school on the other side of the bay—he'd had private tutors before at the spaceship house—and we kept in touch. Sometimes we'd get together in San Francisco or Oakland, and once in a while, we went up to the forest with our parents to visit Lyndon and Penelope and her animals. There were still moments when he acted like a spoiled jerk, but most of the time he was pretty fun to hang out with.

I knew he didn't think he was better than me, because he told me so. A couple months after the fire, as we were following his new bodyguard, Oleg, into a movie theater for a Saturday matinee, he said, "You know, I couldn't have done what you did during the fire. You were smarter than all the adults and braver than everybody."

Then he added, "Do you want some popcorn?"

He acted like it was nothing, but I think he'd been saving up that big speech for a while, timing it just right so I couldn't make a big deal out of it. That was okay by me. I knew he was still getting the hang of the whole being-nice thing. We got our snacks and went into the movie, and I felt like it didn't really matter if I ever beat him in a challenge again.

Although of course I did.

Predictably, the truce between Reynold, Lyndon, and Penelope didn't last for long, and even though Blake didn't talk about it much, it sounded like the fighting wasn't going to end anytime soon. Rich people are ridiculous. I felt sorry for them, honestly. I mean, nobody's family is perfect, but sometimes they're all we've got. And after getting to know the Bertholds, I realized Blake's life was a lot weirder than mine.

We salvaged lots of unobtanium from the house in the forest. Trent used some of it to build new things, and Leya used some of it for her next big art project, which was basically a display of melted electronics on scorched tree stumps. An art gallery loved it and gave her a big show. But because we had permission to use all that stuff, it wasn't as much fun as getting it the old way.

I did take one thing for myself, though, something nobody knew about. One day, while we were digging through the wreckage of Blake's house, I found a twisted lump of metal where the front door used to be. After cleaning the ashes off, I realized what it was: the locking mechanism that had trapped us inside the house until Lyndon chopped his way in. The fire had burned so hot that it was almost unrecognizable, but the metal had melted into a really cool shape, and I decided it was a sculpture formed by the catastrophe. It was a symbol of what happens when you keep people out but also when you let them in. And it was a reminder of the scariest day and the biggest adventure of my life.

It also made a perfect doorstop when I wanted to prop open the door to my bedroom. Because, for the first time ever, I had my own room. And sometimes I even missed Santi.

ACKNOWLEDGMENTS

This book has its origins in my childhood and a night I slept beneath redwood trees outside a trailer belonging to my family's sculptor friend. (Yes, there were spiderwebs on me when I woke up!) But the specific idea of setting a story in Northern California was born during school visits to Montclair Elementary (Oakland), Corpus Christi (Piedmont), Thornhill Elementary (Oakland), and especially the magical Canyon School in the enchanting community of Canyon—my thanks to the students, teachers, and librarians at all four. I'm grateful to Esperanza Surls for giving me a guided tour of the hand-hewn homes of Canyon and bookseller extraordinaire Kathleen Caldwell of A Great Good Place for Books for repeatedly providing a warm welcome to this author.

The first draft of this book was completed shortly before the terrible Camp Fire of November 2018, and I've watched in alarm as fires have become more frequent and destructive throughout the Golden State. While Dagmar's adventures are fictional, too many people have lost their homes for real—and their experiences are terrifying, not thrilling. My heart goes out to all the young readers and their families who have been threatened or displaced by wildfires.

This book was shaped by Kate Meltzer and Stephanie Pitts, two terrifically talented editors at G. P. Putnam's Sons Books for Young Readers. Copy editor Ana Deboo did a wonderful job of whittling away at my linguistic tics, and Kaitlin Kneafsey continues to provide welcome support to my books in the wild. Sheila Hennessey again deserves appreciation for all she has done over the years.

I would like to thank my agent, Josh Getzler, for helping my books find the perfect homes—whether huge or tiny—and Jonathan Cobb for his always timely assistance.

Above all, I'm grateful to my wife, Marya, our sons, Felix and Cosmo, and my furry muses, Toothless and Totoro.

And YOU for reading this book!

READ ON
FOR MORE FROM KEIR GRAFF

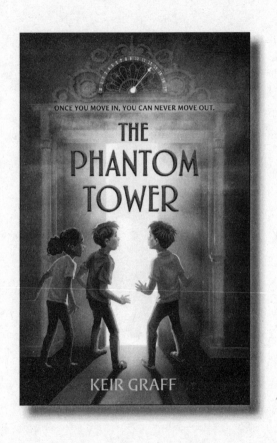

CHAPTER ONE
CHICAGO

THE FIRST TIME I saw Brunhild Towers was the day we moved in. Even though it wasn't that long ago, I saw a lot of things differently back then. I thought old people were boring. I thought learning history was a good way to fall asleep. I thought dying was simple.

You probably noticed I said *Towers*, not *Tower*.

Pay attention and I'll explain everything.

• • •

Mom had been driving all day with my brother, Mal, and me in the back seat. The air conditioner in our old van barely worked, and the August heat was making us sweaty, tired, and crabby. My right arm was red and sore from where Mal had been punching it, and Mal's left arm looked even worse—I was better at using my knuckles.

Mom's voice was fried from telling us to knock it off. Every few miles she tried again.

"Malcolm. Stop arguing."

"Malcolm! Stop hitting!"

"MALCOLM! If you make me pull over and stop this car, you'll lose all your screen time for a week!"

She was talking to both of us, actually. You see, Mal's full name is Malachy, and my name is Colm. Whenever we're in trouble, Mom drops the *and* between our names and we become Malcolm.

The screen-time threat was the only one that worked. Mal's favorite thing is building stuff in *Minecraft*, and mine is wrecking stuff in video games—Mal says I'm just a griefer, but I prefer to think of myself as a demolition expert—so the idea of being grounded from screens after we finally got out of the car was a nightmare.

Still, I just don't think there's any way you can put twin brothers in the back of a minivan for the 926-mile drive from Dallas to Chicago without both of them needing to throw a few punches.

After two days on the road, we were positively sick of each other. We were sick of the way the upholstery rubbed against our sweaty legs, and we were even sick of fast food. All my favorite foods come from drive-through windows, but if I had to unwrap one more burger or breakfast sandwich, I was going to projectile vomit all over our minivan, and we would need to call in a hazmat team to make it habitable again.

The van was so full of stuff, it was almost impossible to move. The space behind us was crammed with boxes. Our feet were resting on duffel bags full of clothes, so we couldn't even straighten our legs, and we had to hit each other over Eric the cat, whose carrier was on the seat between us. The front passenger seat had a lamp, a computer, and our TV in it, which was strapped into the seat belt to protect it from disaster.

If you're wondering why our dad wasn't in that seat, well, it's because he's dead. He was in a car accident two years ago, when Mal and I were ten. Dad was the one who named the cat Eric, but I still don't know why. I've asked him, but he just laughs.

I know what you're thinking: I'm crazy, because you can't talk to dead people. But you're wrong. You *can* talk to them. You're only crazy if you expect them to answer you. I talk to Dad all the time, just to hear his voice in my head. Who cares if I'm making up all the stuff he says? Even so, sometimes I'm afraid he'll stop answering.

Sometimes I'm afraid I'll forget what his voice sounded like.

Moving was Mom's idea. She never even asked what we thought about it. One day, she just told us it was time for a fresh start. She said she had gotten a new job in Chicago and we were leaving in the middle of August. I didn't want to go. I wanted things to stay the same, but it seemed like ever since the policemen came to our door the day Dad didn't come home from work, our old life had been falling apart piece by piece.

Mal didn't like to talk about moving, or Dad, and I hated making Mom cry, so Dad was pretty much the only one I had to talk to.

...

Chicago traffic made Dallas traffic look minor league. It took us an hour and a half to get from the big green *Welcome to Chicago* sign above the highway to our new apartment.

By then, the sun was going down, and I was so hungry that I might even have been able to eat a cheeseburger without spraying it all over the back seat.

Finally, we turned right, and Mom swore and hit the brakes. She swears sometimes, but Mal and I act like we don't hear it. If we swear, that's a different story. She can hear it a block away.

"There it is: Brunhild Tower," she said. "I missed it!"

Then, instead of going around the block like a normal person, Mom backed right down the street, ignoring all the honking horns, while Mal and I scrunched down in our seats and tried to hide. Eric moaned like he was embarrassed, too.

When Mom pulled into the driveway, I couldn't see much—all the stuff crammed into the van blocked the view. But I could tell it was old and fancy: Through the windshield, I glimpsed gray stone, big windows, and some flowers and plants, if you care about that kind of thing.

Mom stopped in front of four tall gray pillars and climbed out of the car.

"Wait here and don't try anything," she said. "I'll just check in with the doorman."

When we heard the word *doorman*, Mal and I exchanged a look. In our old house, you had to jiggle the key in the lock forever before it worked. And in the apartment we moved into after Dad died, we had to enter a key code to get into the building. But we had never lived in a building with a doorman.

"Maybe Mom's new job pays a lot better than her old one," said Mal.

"Who knows?" I said. "She wouldn't even tell us if she won the lottery."

Mom never talked about money. I knew things were tighter now that Dad was gone, but it wasn't like we were rich or anything before that. Still, Mom always tried to act like everything was just great. Like she didn't mind working a part-time job in the evenings and like having a giant old box of a TV was somehow better than having a flat screen like everyone else. Like it was somehow better for Mal and me not to have cell phones when the fact was we just couldn't afford them.

Mal usually went along with her and pretended, but it drove me crazy. It's embarrassing not to have a cell phone or a flat-screen TV. We were lucky our computer wasn't made out of wood.

Mom came out of the building with a man wearing a black-and-gray uniform. The man pointed at something behind us, and Mom got back in the car.

"Who's that?" I asked.

"That's the doorman, dummy," said Mal, taking advantage of my being distracted to hit my arm right on the bruised spot.

I had my fist raised to retaliate when Mom stopped me with a look. So I sent him a telepathic message instead: *I'll get you later.*

"His name is Virgilio," said Mom. "He said there's parking behind us. We can't bring our boxes through the front door—we have to go to the loading dock. But I think it's too late to unload, don't you?"

"Yes," we said at the same time, not wanting anything to get between us and dinner.

We had to drive back onto the street to get to the parking lot. Fortunately, this time, there were only a couple of honks. The way people in Chicago laid on their horns, you'd think they drove horn-powered cars.

Inside the lot, Mom parked in the numbered space Virgilio had given her. Then we got out of the van and stretched. Mom started pulling things out of the back while Mal and I had a quick kickboxing battle that I totally won.

"Malcolm, *enough!*" snapped Mom, holding out things for us to carry.

We took our duffel bags, backpacks, the cat carrier, and the litter box and headed across the lot to the main building.

Brunhild Tower loomed over us, huge and dark. Above the gray stone on the first few floors of the L-shaped building, black iron fire escapes zigzagged up the redbrick walls that faced the parking lot. It was so big,

I felt like it would swallow us up. Suddenly, a stupid hope occurred to me: What if we couldn't find our apartment? Since we weren't unloading the van, we could just drive back to Dallas.

It was still hot as an oven outside. The heat coming off the blacktop practically melted the bottoms of my sneakers. I'm no expert on big cities, but it did seem weird that there was room for such a big parking lot when there were so many tall buildings crowded around.

Mom stood there for a moment, staring up at the building with that look she gets that makes me think she's going to start crying.

"Your dad would have loved this place," she said. "He always liked older buildings. He said they were built to last."

I tried sending Mal a telepathic message: *Quick, change the subject.*

"Why is it called Brunhild Tower?" he asked. Studying his face, I couldn't tell if he'd gotten my message. He probably just asked because he's always going out of his way to learn things he'll never need to know.

"I have no idea," said Mom, snapping out of it. "But it sounds like something out of an old folktale, doesn't it? *Brunhild.*"

"Sounds like a witch's name," I muttered as we started walking toward the building.

None of us had any idea how close Mom and I were to being right.

CHAPTER TWO

BRUNHILD TOWER

VIRGILIO THE DOORMAN seemed like a pretty nice guy. He was short and wide, with jet-black hair, round eyes, a flat nose, and the widest smile I had ever seen.

"Welcome to Brunhild Tower!" he said, grinning and shaking my hand as I came into the little entry room behind Mom.

Then, when Mal appeared behind me, he exclaimed, "Wow—there are two of you!"

People always say a lot of dumb stuff when they meet identical twins, like, "I must be seeing double!" or "When they made you, I guess they *didn't* break the mold!" Fortunately, Virgilio moved on before Mal and I had to decide which one of us would pretend to laugh at the joke.

"So, how old are you guys?" he asked as he shook Mal's hand, too.

"Twelve," I told him.

"So that's . . . what grade?"

"We're going into seventh," said Mal.

"Do you guys like football? Are you going to watch the Chicago Bears?"

"Mal's a mathlete," I told Virgilio. "And he's into *Minecraft*."

"What's your sport? Baseball? Basketball? Hockey?"

I didn't really know how to answer. Dad was a big rugby fan and used to tell us all about it—and we used to play soccer, but since he died, Mom had been too busy to sign us up for teams.

"He likes messing with the things I build in *Minecraft*," said Mal.

Still looking confused, Virgilio asked, "Which one of you is older?"

Now, *that* is an annoying question people always ask twins. I mean, just because I'm one and a half minutes younger, suddenly *I'm* the little brother? It's a meaning-less distinction, and the last thing Mal needs is encouragement.

"I am," said Mal, grinning and poking himself with a thumb.

"By, like, ninety seconds," I added, elbowing him in the ribs.

"And how do people tell you apart?" asked Virgilio.

Mom smiled. "They can't. That's the problem."

"Not even you?"

"It depends," said Mom. "If I've been with them

9

for a while, I can always tell. But if one of them walks into the room and I forget what they've been wearing, sometimes it even takes me a minute."

And if we swapped clothes, I thought, *like we sometimes used to do before Dad died, she had no clue at all.*

Mal looked at me and smiled, like he was remembering the same thing.

"Okay, final question," said Virgilio. "Can you read each other's minds?"

"No," said Mal, at the exact same moment I said, "Yes."

"You guys need to get your story straight," chuckled Virgilio.

Oh, we will, I thought at both of them—but nobody heard me. Lots of twins have reported unusual psychic connections, from being able to read each other's minds and finish each other's sentences to just knowing how the other one is feeling. I knew Mal and I could have this power, too, if he stopped being so uptight about it and let me read his mind. But he kept it zipped up like a winter coat.

The building manager was gone for the day, and Mom had to sign something before Virgilio could give us the keys to our new apartment. Once that was done, he told us which elevator to use and then opened the inner lobby door that let us into the building itself.

It was nice having someone open the door for us, but it was also kind of strange how we had to wait for him to do it. It made me feel special but also a little bit rude.

When I whispered that to Mom, she agreed. "But it's also his job," she said. "So we should let him do it and respect the way he earns his living."

The little entryway where we'd been talking was nice enough, but the actual lobby was super fancy. There was an old fireplace right in front of us, with two chairs and a small table, and tall halls going off to the left and right. Glass chandeliers hung from the ceiling, and there were paintings of lakes, rivers, and prairies on the walls.

My first thought was that it looked like a hotel out of some old movie. A really old-fashioned hotel. I mean, where else do you see furniture in the hallway?

My second thought was, *There's more than one elevator?*

"Virgilio said to turn left and then it would be on the right," said Mom.

We turned left and looked right, down a long hall with evening light coming in through high windows on our left. We walked to the end of the hall and found an elevator. A small metal plate next to the elevator said *01-02*.

"That's not right," said Mom, shaking her head. "Our apartment number is 1404. We're in the wrong tier."

"Tier? What's that?" asked Mal.

Like I said, Mal has to know *everything*.

"There are three elevators in this building, and each elevator serves two apartments on each floor. Each stack of apartments is a tier. We must have walked past ours."

We retraced our steps and found another elevator

where we'd first turned right. The place was so elegant that even the elevators blended into the scenery.

The metal plate beside the doors read *03-04*.

"That's it," said Mom. "We walked right past it."

I pushed the button and looked up to see a semicircle of brass numbers just above the doors. After a moment, an arrow started moving counterclockwise through the numbers as the elevator started to come down.

"I know what you're thinking," I told Mal.

"You do not," he said.

I did know what he was thinking at that moment, though, even if he wasn't transmitting his thoughts: He was missing our old place, where he knew where everything was and how it all worked. With its tiers and hidden elevators, Brunhild Tower was completely different from our old apartment building. But I knew he was also starting to feel a little bit curious about our new home.

Just like I was.

"I know what *I'm* thinking: I can't believe we got this apartment, especially on such short notice," said Mom. "All the other places were smaller and more expensive. It was so nice of my new boss to give me a recommendation."

The elevator doors opened. It sounded like there was an old-fashioned bell trying to ring, but something was stuffed inside. Instead of *DING* it went *TINK*.

"How many floors are in this building, Mom?" I asked as the doors closed behind us.

"Check out the buttons, stupid," said Mal, nodding at the panel next to the doors.

I punched him in the arm and then looked. The highest button was labeled *17*.

"Seventeen floors," I said. "What's our apartment number again?"

"1404," said Mom.

"We are going to have a rockstar view," said Mal.

I looked at the buttons again and pushed *14*. Then I noticed something weird: The button below ours was *12*.

The elevator doors closed, and we started going up.

"There's no 13," I told Mal and Mom.

"People used to be superstitious about the number 13," said Mom. "They thought it was unlucky."

"That's called triskaidekaphobia," said Mal with a smug smile on his face.

I thought about punching him just for knowing that but decided to save it for something more annoying. Because it *was* kind of an interesting word.

"They would leave out the number thirteen whenever they could," continued Mom. "Most old buildings don't have a thirteenth floor."

"Well, they do—" I started to say.

"But they're numbered fourteen," said Mal.

I glared at him. When Mal finished my sentences, it wasn't because he was reading my mind. It was because he couldn't help interrupting me.

"So when you think about it, we're on the thirteenth floor," Mal explained, just to make sure we all knew he had figured it out.

"I guess you're right, Mal," said Mom. "It's a good thing we're not superstitious."

Speak for yourself, I thought. I'm not afraid of unlucky numbers, but I still think there are a lot of things we don't know, if you know what I mean.

The elevator stopped, and the doors opened with that same *TINK*. We stepped out into a short hall with doors on the right and left. There was a lamp on a table, and four framed pictures on the wall showed what looked like Chicago in the olden days.

"I don't know if this is a room or a hallway," I said.

"It's called an elevator lobby," said Mom. "It's like a waiting area for these two apartments."

Right then, Eric meowed really loud.

"Better hurry—I think he has to use the litter box," said Mal.

Mom unlocked the top lock, then the bottom lock, and pushed the heavy front door open. She turned on the lights, and we squeezed past her and ran into the apartment. I put down the cat carrier and took a look around.

CHAPTER THREE
APARTMENT 1404

THE FIRST THING we noticed was that the place was *huge*. In our last apartment, you could practically see the whole thing as soon as you walked in. Here, all I could see were halls and doors.

"Slow down, guys!" laughed Mom, opening the door of the carrier so Eric could come out.

But we were already running around, turning on all the lights, going down the hallway to the right (where there were two bedrooms and two bathrooms) and the hallways to the left (where we found the kitchen, an empty room, another bathroom, and a hallway to the dining room) before finally working our way back around to the giant living room. The view stopped us in our tracks.

It was a corner room, and out the windows on one wall, we could see a harbor, a park, and the dark water of Lake Michigan with the setting sun making the clouds glow pink. Out of the windows on another wall, we could see white headlights and red taillights as cars sped along a highway Mom said was called Lake Shore Drive. In the distance, a crowd of skyscrapers shot straight up, their windows sparkling with light.

The view was so distracting, it took me a while to notice something else about our new apartment: It was full of other people's furniture. There were couches and chairs in the living room, a table and chairs in the dining room, lamps in the corners, and even paintings on the wall.

"Are you sure this is the right apartment?" I asked. "It's full of someone else's stuff."

"This apartment comes furnished," said Mom. "And even if we hadn't sold our old furniture at the yard sale, we barely would have had enough to fill one room of this place—it's so big."

Unlike the furniture in the lobby downstairs, the couches and chairs in the apartment didn't look like they came from a hotel. They looked like they came from someone's house. The cushions were so flat you could practically imagine people sitting in them, and there were a couple of stains that made you wonder if they were sloppy eaters.

It wasn't nice and new. It was weird and old.

"It smells funny," I said.

"Nothing a little fresh air won't fix," said Mom cheerfully.

"Let's open the windows!" said Mal, of course going along with her.

"Though it would be nice if this place had air-conditioning," added Mom.

We went around opening windows and letting in hot, humid air—along with some big spiders that had made giant webs on the outside of the windows. We flung them back outside with a newspaper, and then we washed our hands in the bathrooms, which looked like they were a hundred years old.

When I turned on the faucet to wash my hands, what came out was a reddish-brown liquid. It looked like blood.

"MOM!" I yelled.

When she poked her head around the corner, I pointed at the sink.

"I think this place is haunted," I said.

"Oh, that's just rust in the pipes," said Mom. "Let it run a minute; it'll be fine. Old buildings are full of surprises."

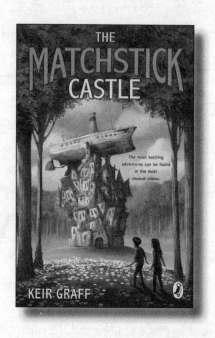

"For boys and girls alike, this story sings."
—Blue Balliett, award-winning author of *Chasing Vermeer*

"A compelling reminder that it's a great big world out there,
just waiting for the next generation of dreamers and explorers."
—*Chicago Tribune*

"This quirky novel is reminiscent of a
Wes Anderson movie for the tweenage set."
—*School Library Journal*

"A whimsical adventure with a large dose of humor."
—Jennifer Chambliss Bertman, bestselling author
of the Book Scavenger series

"Fast-paced, anarchic fun for reluctant and avid readers alike."
—*Kirkus Reviews*

"A zippy, adventurous romp in the woods."
—*The Bulletin of the Center for Children's Books*